WHEN GOOD EARLS GO BAD

By Megan Frampton

When Good Earls Go Bad (A Novella)
The Duke's Guide to Correct Behavior

When Good Earls Go Bad

A Victorian Valentine's Day Novella

Megan Frampton

AVONIMPULSE
An Imprint of HarperCollinsPublishers

Excerpt from *Put Up Your Duke* copyright © 2015 by Megan Frampton.

Excerpt from *Various States of Undress: Georgia* copyright © 2014 by Laura Simcox.

Excerpt from *Make It Last* copyright © 2014 by Megan Erickson.

Excerpt from *Hero By Night* copyright © 2014 by Sara Jane Stone.

Excerpt from *Mayhem* copyright © 2014 by Jamie Shaw.

Excerpt from *Sinful Rewards 1* copyright © 2014 by Cynthia Sax.

Excerpt from *Forbidden* copyright © 2014 by Charlotte Stein.

Excerpt from *Her Highland Fling* copyright © 2014 by Jennifer McQuiston.

EPub Edition FEBRUARY 2015 ISBN: 9780062380319

Print Edition ISBN: 9780062380302

AM 10 9 8 7 6 5 4

A Belle's Guide to Household Management

When you are asked to dust the furniture, do not make the mistake of bringing dust in and placing it on the furniture; the order is, in fact, to un-dust the furniture. This will save you many hours of dust-locating, placing, and then un-dusting.

CHAPTER ONE

"While it's not precisely true that nobody is here, because I am, in fact, here, the truth is that there is no one here who can accommodate the request."

The man standing in the main area of the Quality Employment Agency didn't leave. She'd have to keep on, then.

"If I weren't here, then it would be even more in question, since you wouldn't know the answer to the question one way or the other, would you? So I am here, but I am not the proper person for what you need."

The man fidgeted with the hat he held in his hand. But still did not take her hint. She would have to persevere.

"I suggest you leave the information, and we will endeavor to fill the position when there is someone here who is not me." Annabelle gave a short nod of her head as she finished speaking, knowing she had been absolutely clear in what she'd said. If repetitive. So it was a surprise that the man to whom she was speaking was staring back at her, his mouth slightly opened, his eyes blinking behind his owlish spectacles. His hat now held very tightly in his hand.

Perhaps she should speak more slowly.

"We do not have a housekeeper for hire," she said, pausing between each word. "I am the owner, not one of the employees for hire."

Now the man's mouth had closed, but it still seemed as though he did not understand.

"I do not understand," he said, confirming her very suspicion. "This is an employment agency, and I have an employer who wishes to find an employee. And if I do not find a suitable person within…"—and at this he withdrew a pocket watch from his waistcoat and frowned at it, as though it was its fault it was already past tea time, and *goodness, wasn't she hungry and had Caroline left any milk in the jug? Because if not, well*—"twenty-four hours, my employer, the Earl of Selkirk, will be most displeased, and we will ensure your agency will no longer receive our patronage."

That last part drew her attention away from the issue of the milk and whether or not there was any.

"The Earl of…?" she said, feeling that flutter in her stomach that signaled there was nobility present or being mentioned—or she wished there were, at least. Rather like the milk, actually.

"Selkirk," the man replied in a firm tone. He had no comment on the milk. And why would he? He didn't even know it was a possibility that they didn't have any, and if she did have to serve him tea, what would she say? Besides which, she had no clue to the man's name; he had just come in and been all brusque and demanded a housekeeper when there was none.

"Selkirk," Annabelle repeated, her mind rifling through all the nobles she'd ever heard mentioned.

"A Scottish earl," the man said.

Annabelle beamed and clapped her hands. "Oh, Scottish! Small wonder I did not recognize the title, I've only ever been in London and once to the seaside when I was five years old, but I wouldn't have known if that was Scotland, but I am fairly certain it was not because it would have been cold and it was quite warm in the water. Unless the weather was unseasonable, I can safely say I have never been to Scotland, nor do I know of any Scottish earls."

"Glad to have that settled," the man said in the kind of strangled hush that most people seemed to speak after some time conversing with her. "The thing is, the purpose of my visit here is to hire a person to take care of the earl while he is in London on business."

Annabelle opened her mouth to speak, but he held his hand up, indicating she should wait.

That, too, was something many people did to her. Was there a class that everyone took in How to Speak to Annabelle of which she was unaware? Because they were remarkably consistent in their discourse, and it couldn't be coincidental.

But he was still speaking, so she couldn't think about the possibility of the class, and whether she herself would be allowed to enroll. And why they hadn't asked her to lead the class.

"And the earl was most specific, as he is about most things," the man said, almost as though he were annoyed about that, "that there be someone at the house he's rented to prepare it for his arrival. I do not have time to waste on this matter. Do you have a housekeeper who can take care of the earl for the time, perhaps as much as a month, that he is in residence in London?"

He drew himself up to his full height and stared down at her, as though daring her to reply in a way he did not want.

"To be clear," he continued, as though he hadn't been clear already. Only she still wasn't quite certain, so perhaps he hadn't. "To be clear, the earl is most insistent that he only have a housekeeper while he is in residence." His expression revealed just what he thought of that edict. "So can you assist, or should I apply to another agency?"

Annabelle liked to accommodate, and the earl was an earl, after all. Even if she could already tell he was odd, not only because he was Scottish but because he wasn't demanding that every servant in London bow to his every whim.

She bit her lip and thought about it for perhaps half a second, almost the same amount of time she spent on what she was going to say next in general. Her agency partner had been just as reckless a few months ago, and look where that had gotten her: a duke for a husband and a new child without the bother of childbirth.

This would not net her a duke, obviously, since this was an earl, and she hoped that there were not any children going to be in residence, but still, besides all that, it was a remarkably similar situation.

"I do not normally take on positions myself, you understand, but since the earl is in such desperate need, and there is no one here"—*as I've mentioned several times, you'd think he could have realized that by now*—"who can fill the situation, I will come along and take care of it. For a month, no longer." That would bring her up to right around Valentine's Day, and if she were busy, perhaps she wouldn't remember she did not have a Valentine. "Is that suitable?"

Now the man—she might have to ask his name soon, only then she might also have to offer him tea, since they had become known to one another, and she still hadn't figured out the milk issue—had what she might call a smirk on his face, only she didn't know him well enough to know if he was amused or he was perhaps hungry. In which case she'd have to offer him tea, damn the milk, and she really did not want to do that. Mostly because she now had to find out where the Scottish earl lived and get over there to discover what needed doing.

It likely included buying milk.

"You," he said, and now she knew he wasn't hungry, he was amused, because there was a strong hint of a laugh in his tone, only she didn't see what there was that was so funny. "You would be perfect. Thank you."

It wasn't very long after she'd closed the door behind Mr. Bell—she'd found out his name, as well as his employment at a London-based company that had a Scottish name, only she couldn't remember what it was—and left a note for Caroline, the other owner of the agency, that she had gone to her lodgings and packed a bag with all the essentials she'd require for being away for a month: her gowns, the good one and the better one (she left the best at home since she didn't think she'd need it and she was wearing the worst one), all of the installments of Mr. Dickens's *Pickwick Papers*, and her feather duster, which hadn't seen much use as its intended function, but it was colorful and might make her look more officially like a housekeeper.

She couldn't bring Cat, her cat (*obviously!*), since she didn't think the earl would appreciate a feline being sprung at him, even if Cat was way too timid to spring at anyone, but likely the earl wouldn't care about Cat's lack of confidence; he would just be irked that she had brought an inhabitant to the house who was neither a housekeeper nor an earl.

Imagine, after all, if he didn't even want anything but a housekeeper, not even a cook or a scullery maid or anything. He definitely would not want a cat in the house, even if it was Cat. Just the housekeeper, and it sounded as though he didn't even want that. Her, that is.

Not that *she* was a housekeeper, but she would endeavor to keep that secret to herself. Although Mr. Bell likely suspected, given that she had basically told him that. But he didn't seem to mind—or possibly he didn't understand?—so hopefully the earl wouldn't. Mind or understand, that is. And even if she wasn't technically a housekeeper, she wouldn't let the house go, so she wasn't a housegiverawayer or anything, so if she could just ensure the house was kept, she felt certain, confident even, that he would never know.

So Cat was currently ensconced with her landlady, who promised to feed Cat on a schedule (*if "constant" was a schedule*), and Annabelle was trudging up Grove End Road, her valise in hand and her annoyance at herself for being such an avid reader (the papers were heavy) in her head.

Thankfully No. 65 arrived soon after No. 63, and she drew out the key Mr. Bell had given her and inserted it into the lock of the door.

The door swung wide and emitted an ominous creaking noise that made Annabelle's heart flutter against her ribs.

And not in the pleasant *I've just thought about nobility* way. Because this nobility was Scottish, after all, and she had no idea what their type of nobility was like.

She took a deep breath and stepped over the threshold.

And stood in the small hallway, a torrent of dust billowing up from the floor as though she were some sort of Celtic warrior woman and the dust was her army.

Although she would have to eradicate the dust, wouldn't she, given that she was now a housekeeper and not a housegiverawayer. So did that make her a Celtic warrior traitor? Never mind. She'd solve all that later.

The house was so still and the dust so present, it was clear no one had stood in this hallway for a long while. Mr. Bell had said the earl would arrive tomorrow and that he only required a few rooms for his visit, and thankfully it was early enough today—*or earl-y, she snickered to herself*—so she could attack her Dust Army and perhaps brave the kitchen to ensure there were no Mice Minions lurking in there to disturb her.

She did miss Cat.

The house wasn't small, of course, it was a residence fit for an earl, but it wasn't overly large either, so perhaps it wouldn't be too difficult for even a nonhousekeeper to straighten up a few rooms.

From the way it sounded, having even a housekeeper was a concession. Perhaps the earl didn't eat. Or make any sort of mess. Or speak with people.

Or maybe he liked doing all the cooking and cleaning himself, although that would make him remarkably different from any other members of the nobility she'd heard of. Mostly noblemen liked to talk to other noblemen and look at attractive women. She'd never heard anything about their liking to cook or clean.

But all this pondering about who the earl might be or what he wanted, was not going to get done what she wanted, which was removing the Dust Army so there was just warrior Annabelle.

Leaving the valise in the hall, she went through each of the rooms on the ground floor—sitting room, dining room, pantry, and a music room. Downstairs was the kitchen, which you could get to only by descending a small narrow staircase. The kitchen itself was dusty, but did not appear to have mice, and was relatively tidy if not precisely clean.

So, she would do the main hallway, the kitchen, and her own bedroom. She'd save the earl's bedroom for the morning; there would be plenty of time to take care of it, then.

She returned to the ground floor, then hoisted her valise up and walked up the staircase to the first floor. As expected, the hallway opened onto a variety of bedrooms, with the largest one at the back of the house where it was presumably the most quiet. Again, while the rooms were neat, there was a massive amount of dust, and Annabelle had to take her kerchief from her gown and tie it over her nose and mouth so as not to breathe in too much of the dust. She put her valise into the smallest bedroom, then headed back downstairs to find cleaning implements and hopefully not very many mice.

Hours later, Annabelle was exhausted, but the hallway and the kitchen had been vanquished, at least, as had her worst gown, which would need its own cleaning to regain its title of worst; right now it was definitely the Most Worst, and that was putting it kindly. The kitchen had taken the longest, and she really did hope he didn't want to eat much, because if she never set foot in that kitchen again she would be a happy woman.

Not that she wasn't happy now, of course. Or rather, not that she wasn't fine. That's what she said whenever anyone asked how she was—"fine." Fine with being a fallen woman who was trying to get up, fine with working at the agency with her best friends, fine with having no one to lavish love on besides Cat, fine with ruining her worst dress if it meant snagging an earl for a client. Fine with all of that, and fine with being so bone tired she was almost glad there was no food, because now she could just take herself off to bed without worrying about eating. There would be time to eat tomorrow, before the earl arrived at midday. As well as clean his bedroom. She'd shut the doors to all the bedrooms on the first floor but the small one she'd claimed for her own; there was no bedroom off the kitchen, which was the normal place for a housekeeper to sleep, she knew, but she was secretly relieved because of the potential for mouseness with no Cat.

Meanwhile, her bed was calling. Well, no, actually it wasn't, because wouldn't that be an odd thing, if an inanimate object called out to her? And if that happened, what else would speak? Probably her shoes would chime in and complain about how much time she spent wearing them. And it was impossible to even imagine the endless complaints the teakettle would have: *I'm hot, I'm cold, I'm empty, I'm full, make your mind up already.* It was better, then, that nothing called out to her.

Except the bed, which she was absolutely fine with answering.

Annabelle walked wearily upstairs, holding the railing as though it were propping her up. The room she'd chosen as her own was...*fine*, the walls papered with blue wallpaper that had birds and flowers on it. It was pretty, and for a moment, Annabelle wished she could just fly into the wallpaper and take up residence there. It would be so much easier than all of this work.

But there'd be no Caroline or Lily, who was now the duchess, or the agency—or even Cat. Or if there were Cat, Cat would make it his mission to eat her if she were a bird in wallpaper. So being a bird in wallpaper was not that good an idea after all.

She drew off her absolute worst possible gown and dropped it on the floor—the floor was likely cleaner than the gown—and then removed her corset and dropped that on top of the gown, leaving her in her shift.

She was too tired to unearth her nightgown, so she just opened the covers and crawled in, feeling herself fall asleep almost as soon as her head hit the pillow.

A Belle's Guide to Household Management

A housekeeper is similar to a man (even though she is always a woman!): She needs to know everything about a particular subject without ever having to do it herself.

CHAPTER TWO

If there was one thing that Matthew, Earl of Selkirk, despised more than being late, it was being early.

"We're here, my lord," the cabbie said, his accent dropping half of the consonants as though they were not fit to be mentioned.

Being early meant there was wasted time. Matthew hated to waste time. If he'd been late, chances were that some required work had delayed him; being early just meant he had not planned properly.

In this particular case, he had not planned properly so much as to make him early by half a day. He could have spent that time doing more research into his uncle's bank or reviewing his own accounts or translating more of the works he'd found in the attic into current language or any number of interesting things.

He would not be entering a rented house in London at eight o'clock in the evening.

He stepped out of the carriage onto the street, the streetlights making it nearly as bright as daytime. A waste of money, surely, and if there was one thing Matthew hated as much as being late or being early, it was wasting money. Were London's inhabitants so delicate they couldn't find their way in the dark?

Not to mention, likely any English earl wouldn't worry about being late or early; whenever he arrived would be the proper time. But Matthew wasn't English, he was Scottish, and despite what the earls in England might do, Matthew worked. And didn't have much respect for anyone who didn't work, not if they could do some good and keep themselves busy. Even though that also meant he didn't always have respect for his fellow Scottish lords.

"Sure you don't want me to carry your trunk in, my lord?" the cabbie said, looking skeptically at either Matthew or the trunk, Matthew wasn't sure.

Not that it mattered.

"No, thank you," he said, reaching into his pockets for the fare. "Here you go."

The cabbie looked at what Matthew had given him and raised his head, scowling. "Scottish, are you?"

As though the man could not tell by Matthew's accent.

"Yes, Scottish." This was not the time to discuss one's origins. It was late, even though he was early, and Matthew's trunk still remained on the back of the cab. "If you don't mind?" he said, gesturing to the trunk.

The man shook his head, as though in disgust, and hauled the trunk off the back of the cab onto the sidewalk. He didn't even look at Matthew before vaulting up onto the seat of the cab, uttering some inarticulate grunt to get his horse moving.

Matthew felt in his waistcoat pocket for the key Mr. Bell had given him, checking for perhaps the thousandth time that day. Reassured, he bent down to the trunk and grabbed the handles on either side.

He'd been traveling all day, sitting on a train, and hadn't gotten his usual exercise of walking, so it felt good to work his muscles. Muscles that felt as though they were perfectly happy to have a day off from what he normally did to them, judging by the twinge that followed as he hoisted the trunk up against his body.

It couldn't be helped, though. The cabbie was long gone, there was no one else on the street, and he'd have felt like an idiot if he had to ask for help anyway. He hated asking for help as much as he hated wasting time. Or money—that, as much as his need for quiet, was what made him only grudgingly accept the necessity of a housekeeper during his stay. He didn't see the point of anything more, anybody more; it would be wasteful to have people around when he was just working. But he had to have someone, that was made painfully clear. But thankfully she wouldn't arrive until tomorrow, so he would have at least twelve hours to himself.

Perhaps there would be a comfortable chair, and if he could just manage to find a glass, he would be able to relax with a bit of whisky before going to bed.

And then tomorrow he would begin to focus on the task at hand.

"Wha' will be a traitor knave? Wha' will fill a something something's grave?" Matthew sang as he downed the last sip of whisky, realizing he hadn't had anything to eat for nearly half a day. That was very poor planning on his part. A definite misstep, and doubtless caused by the whole being-early fracas.

Well, it was far too late for him to go out anywhere. Plus his bed was waiting, and the room was, if not spinning, then a little wobbly around the edges. He definitely couldn't focus enough to read, which was his usual evening pursuit. And he didn't know where the library was anyway, if it was here, and even if he could find it, it probably didn't have what he liked to read.

He glanced around to locate his trunk, which he would have sworn he'd dragged in here. Yes! There it was, just inside the door. But it would be too hard to carry the trunk up the stairs, especially since he also wanted to bring the bottle to bed with him. He looked at the trunk, then the bottle, then the trunk again.

Of course. He could solve this with logic, as he always did. He tucked the bottle under his arm and approached the trunk as though it might rear up and bite him. Then he undid the clasps and flung the lid up.

His nightshirt was right on top, the most logical place for it to be. He congratulated himself, as he often did, on applying logic to even the most minuscule of tasks. It made things so much easier and wasted much less time. Therefore, his nightshirt was on the top, so he could put it on immediately, his toiletries were just below, and so on. He picked the garment up, then tucked it under the same arm that held the whisky bottle. Now for the stairs.

Where were they? Oh, yes, just to the right of the room he was in now. He'd only seen this room and the entryway, but thus far, it seemed like a pleasant house. He had been dreading the thought of coming to London—his first time here, and he had not made the trip willingly—but if he had this place to come home to in the evening, a quiet, restful house, he might escape unscathed by his experience.

The stairs weren't as hard to conquer as he'd thought they might be; true, one of the steps appeared to lunge up at him, but he righted himself at the last minute and was able to maintain control of the bottle.

His nightshirt was not so fortunate, however; as he reached the first floor landing, he noticed a strong aroma of whisky. The bottle had leaked, but it seemed most of it had fallen on the fabric.

Thankfully, there was no chance of anyone seeing him in his bed. It was the most practical decision to sleep naked, so that was what he would do.

He dropped the spirits-soaked garment on the floor of the landing and entered the closest room, the only one with an open door. He'd investigate his new lodgings in the morning; right now he needed to sleep.

Once inside, he drew his jacket off, then his cravat, then drew his shirt over his head. He lowered his hands to his boots, but that was awkward, given his current state of inebriation, so he just sat down on the floor and took them off, then yanked his trousers down.

The moon shone bright through one of the windows, and he was grateful not to have to trust his unsteady hand with a candle. There was plenty of light to see the bed, just there in the corner.

He drew the covers back and slid in, expecting a cold, empty bed.

Instead, he found it to be quite warm, and filled with another occupant.

A Belle's Guide to Household Management

Beating the rug does not mean you engage to trounce the rug in a game of cards.

CHAPTER THREE

Annabelle had never been so comfortable before, or at least it felt that way. The bed was soft and warm, the house was quiet, just a slight rustling of something, fabric maybe? Then the feel of another body easing into—

"What? Who? What are you doing in here?" she said, kicking at the other occupant of the bed, who was not only someone she'd not invited in, but definitely not anyone she'd even ever met before.

It was light enough in the room, thanks to the moonlight, to see it was a man, which did not reassure her. From what she saw of his expression, however, he was just as startled as she was to find her there. Well, she was not startled to find herself there, but she was startled to find him.

Perhaps she would not be the best person to lead the How to Speak to Annabelle course, since she barely understood herself what she was thinking.

"Who are you?" His voice held a foreign accent, but it was his obvious outrage that she listened to the most.

"Who am I?" she said, pushing herself back into the corner of the bed, her back making a comforting contact with the wall. "Who am I? I am supposed to be here, whereas you…"

"Are supposed to be here also," he replied, before she could finish her sentence.

And the foreign accent clicked it all into place, and she felt her stomach whoosh in panic and terror and…

"You're the earl. And you're early."

His face did not change, not even when she stressed "early" as in *earl-y*.

"And who are you?" he said, folding his arms across his— *oh my goodness*—naked chest.

"The housekeeper?" Annabelle hated that her voice rose at the end, as though she weren't quite sure herself. "The housekeeper," she said, this time in a much firmer tone. But not nearly as firm as his chest was; it was rippled throughout with all sorts of intriguing muscles and a light dusting of dark chest hair, and his shoulders were so broad it seemed he filled the room, or at least her vision of the room.

And suddenly she was even warmer in her bed than she'd been five minutes ago.

The Scottish earl should not be this attractive, which she could tell even only by the moonlight. Imagine the impact when she viewed him with the full strength of the sun. She shuddered at the thought, only the shudder somehow seemed to feel more like a shiver. Of something.

"You were not to arrive until tomorrow," he said, his voice, despite the nice Scottish burr, practically dripping disdain.

"Well, I'm here, and so are you, and here we are, and you are nearly, well, if I might say so, you are nearly naked,"

Annabelle finished in a rush, trying very hard not to look there, not where there were some interesting parts covered by his underclothes.

Even in the dim light she could see when he realized just how he must look, his eyebrows raising up so far up his face it seemed as though he might just take flight, his eyes wide.

"Mrs. Housekeeper, I promise you, I am not in the habit of..." he began, then spun on his heels—or his bare feet, actually, since he wasn't wearing boots, presenting Annabelle with a view of a very strong, very broad back, with some even more interesting divots that were on either side of his lower spine.

He picked something up off the floor, then got onto one foot and stuffed his leg into his trousers, followed by the other leg. Then some hasty buttoning of something or another, and then he turned back around, still shirtless, but at least she wasn't distracted by all the white fabric and other things any longer.

Unless she was distracted by the fact she wasn't distracted any longer, and she rather wished she had gotten a chance to see what his legs looked like. She could just imagine, given how he seemed to tower over the bed, that he was very tall, and that his legs were suitably long as well. Because it would just be odd if his legs were only as long as hers were, for example, with him being so much taller than she.

"Perhaps you might join me downstairs, and we can discuss the situation." It was not a request, and what was more, it sounded as though he were about to lecture her on her inadvisable behavior, when really it was he who was inadvised, having gotten into her bed, and not the other way around.

But she didn't point any of that out to him; first of all, his chest was distracting her, he seemed even more naked now that he was half-clothed than when he was nearly entirely naked, which was an odd sort of situation. Plus he was her new employer, and he was an earl, and she was not even a real housekeeper, even if she did own a feather duster.

"Of course, my lord," she said instead, lowering her gaze from his chest to the bed. Definitely a much less distracting view. But also much less intriguing.

"Five minutes," he said as he picked something else up off the floor and walked out of the room.

Leaving her much more awake, intrigued, and surprisingly warm than she had been five minutes earlier.

Matthew stomped downstairs after grabbing his things, including his whisky bottle, from the room, feeling as though he should be apologizing to the stranger in his bed but also as though it was entirely her fault she was in his bed in the first place.

Although perhaps that wasn't his bed? In which case it was his fault. He shook his head; it couldn't be his fault, nothing was. People were just mistaken when they thought it was. And he would have to spend time, time he didn't have, explaining how they were wrong.

It had gotten to the point where his sisters, all four of them, just rolled their eyes and made a *hmphing* sound whenever he opened his mouth. That was one advantage London had—no younger sisters who required watching over.

Although it seemed he had acquired a housekeeper who did. He had been expecting an older, perhaps gray-haired lady, not a young woman with blonde hair and what appeared to be some very nice curves, at least judging by how the comforter she'd clutched around her looked. Not that he had looked.

Having an attractive housekeeper was an unexpected surprise. Matthew did not like unexpected surprises, although not as vehemently as he disliked wasting time or money. This…this was just a minor change in his expectations, and he could change his expectations, despite what his sisters might say.

Thank goodness none of them were here now, or they would be doubled over in laughter at seeing their older brother so nonplussed by this situation.

With that sobering thought in mind, he put his shirt back on and did up the buttons. His cravat was still upstairs; there was no help for it but for his housekeeper to see him not garbed entirely appropriately.

But that just made him realize she had seen him nearly entirely garbed—or not—inappropriately, and an unfamiliar feeling rose up, making him feel flushed, or as though he had a fever.

He certainly hoped he was not catching ill. London was bad enough; to be here and be sick was not at all to be desired. The sooner he was done with his uncle's business, the sooner he could return to Edinburgh, where all the housekeepers, in his experience, were not comely ladies, at least that he'd noticed.

He heard her footsteps on the stairs and turned to her. Yes, she was definitely not what he'd expected.

"My lord," she said with a curtsy. She had gotten dressed and come downstairs all within five minutes. Excellent. That would make up for the fact that she was young, blonde, and, as he could see now, unaccountably pretty. What was she doing being a housekeeper? That was a mystery, and Matthew did not, of course, like mysteries. They always just needed solving and were invariably dull once one had solved them.

Although he might find this mystery more interesting to solve.

"My lord?" she said again in an impatient tone, with a rise at the end of her voice meaning she was waiting for a reply.

Of course. She was. And here he was wondering about the intrigue of his new temporary housekeeper and was just likely wondering when he might respond.

He could take care of that now, at least. "Yes, Mrs.—? What is your name?"

"Annabelle Tyne," she replied. "Of the Quality Employment Agency, and it's Miss Tyne," she added, as though that made a difference.

"Miss Tyne, it appears we have met each other in a rather odd way." *If you consider meeting in bed an odd way, which he hoped she did, otherwise she would not be a suitable housekeeper at all.* "Let us start again. I am Matthew, Earl of Selkirk. And you are Miss Tyne. It is late, and I am more than accustomed to sleeping wherever I happen to find myself, so you may return to the bedroom, and I will sleep down here. We will discuss your duties in the morning. I will be up at six o'clock; I presume you will also."

She nodded, tugging her lip with her teeth. "Yes, my lord, if that is best. I could clean the master bedroom, if you would prefer."

Matthew exhaled. "I do not prefer. If I did prefer, that is what I would have asked you to do. I did not, and therefore you may assume I do not wish for that. I will ask for what I want, I assure you." He realized, as he finished speaking, that what he had said could be an invitation to something other than housecleaning, something he'd never asked before, but something that was suddenly of more interest than it had been before he entered the house.

He could and should not entertain any of those types of thoughts regarding his housekeeper, or any woman, in fact, until he was married. It was not at all suitable for him to think of any woman who was not his wife. Tempted though he was. Or perhaps he was just tempted to touch her because he wished to straighten her hair, which was currently flying about her head in a most unruly cloud.

"I see," she said, an amused tone in her voice. "I will see you in the morning, then, my lord," she added, then dipped a curtsy and walked back upstairs, Matthew doing his best not to watch.

A Belle's Guide to Household Management

Bedclothes are not what YOU wear to bed, but what your bed wears to…bed.

Chapter Four

My goodness, Annabelle thought as she walked upstairs, acutely conscious that he was still down there, perhaps even still looking at her; her new employer was an exceedingly handsome man.

For one thing, she hadn't been wrong before when she noticed he was absurdly tall. Then there were his broad shoulders, his body tapering down into a slim waist and long legs. And his face, which she hadn't gotten a good look at before in the bedroom; it was too dark and she was too distracted by his naked chest.

He was commandingly handsome, with dark hair and eyes and a strong blade of a nose on top of a surprisingly full mouth. That mouth gave him a sensuous look, one at complete odds with his otherwise very serious demeanor. His words were clipped, despite the burr of his accent, and his very manner seemed to insist on obedience. Obedience she was hoping to be able to comply with, or those lovely lips might flatten into a hard line and she'd be sent on her way, without having snagged an earl as an agency client or, for that matter, having gotten a decent night of sleep.

And she would be in proximity to him for a month? Him, with his firm tone, and firmer chest, his intense eyes focused on the work she'd be doing for him?

Suddenly it didn't seem like such a grand idea, taking on a housekeeping job when the only thing she'd managed to keep properly was Cat.

But if she bolted now, she'd have to tell her partners at the agency that she had been intimidated by a naked chest and a handsome earl and a strong, commanding voice. And she'd never get to see more of that chest or find out what could possibly make that mouth smile.

Caroline was always telling her to stay focused, to find a goal and try to achieve it. Usually this was in the context of Annabelle actually remembering to make the tea after she'd boiled the water, but it could be applied to larger things, couldn't it?

So perhaps she should set a goal of not being distracted by the earl. He was definitely larger than a cup of tea. In many ways.

Matthew wasted no time in finishing the rest of the whisky; it made sense to do so now, unlike his having begun to drink too much of it in the first place, since he'd need help sleeping. Then he lay down on the sofa and settled himself to sleep.

Unfortunately, it also made sense he'd have a headache in the morning, so he couldn't blame anyone but himself for how his head ached and how his mouth felt, as though he'd been chewing on cotton.

He got up from the sofa, which wasn't nearly long enough for his six-foot-plus frame, feeling his legs grumble nearly as much as he wished to at having been in a cramped position for most of the night. He heard someone coming down the stairs and hastily pulled his sleeves down and donned his coat. He did not wish to repeat the nearly naked-in-front-of-the-housekeeper experience he'd had the night before.

"Good morning, my lord," he heard her call out, then she entered the room, glancing about the room until she spotted him. At which point she smiled.

Miss Tyne had clearly slept wonderfully, at least judging by her cheery face and bright tone. The thought of her in the bed, the comforter curled around her warm form, was enough to put him in an even worse mood, for no good reason.

"Good morning," Matthew said in a grunt. He cast a surreptitious glance at her from under his lashes—yes, she was as pretty as he'd thought the night before. It was not the result of his imbibing. If anything, she was even more attractive in the bright light of day; her blonde hair, now tidied, caught the sun; her smile, if one were inclined to be prone to infection, was practically infectious; and her warm brown eyes sparkled with humor, as though she were on the verge of telling a joke that would beguile and amuse everyone in her immediate environs.

Matthew did not like jokes.

"Do you need breakfast?" she asked, then continued without waiting for him to answer. "Not that there is any food in the house. I haven't gone shopping yet; I wanted to ascertain if there was anything in particular you wished for." She wrinkled her face up in an expression of thought. "Not that I am a very good cook; in fact about all I can make is tea, oatmeal, toast, and, well, I think that is it. Tea, oatmeal, and toast. And I usually burn the toast."

"But," she went on, walking further into the room, "I can see if the Quality Employment Agency has any cooks on its roster for hire. I know Mr. Bell said you didn't want one, but you have to eat, don't you, and meanwhile, I can make you some tea. Or oatmeal. Or..."

"Or toast," Matthew completed.

"Exactly! You are brilliant," she said in what appeared to be a genuine tone of voice.

Remarkable.

"Although I would have to go out and buy the ingredients, since, as I said, there is nothing here."

"I do not plan on taking many meals at the house, so there is no need for a cook." Matthew felt the rush of frustration that always accompanied his having to explain things. "If I had wanted a cook, I would have instructed Mr. Bell to hire one for me while I am here. I did not. All I need is a housekeeper"—*although I should have specified she be gray-haired and shaped like a dumpling*—"to keep the house relatively clean, answer the door while I am away, and ensure there is clean linen and that my clothes are kept tidy."

She wrinkled her brow again. "No meals? Not even tea? You must have tea," she said, as though his not wanting the hot beverage was an impossibility.

"Fine. Tea. Here," Matthew said, digging in his pockets for change. "Take this and go out and buy tea things. Which way is the kitchen? I'll need to wash up."

Now she looked absolutely startled, and he would be grumpier if she just weren't so...adorable. And where did that word spring from? He didn't think he'd ever thought anyone or anything adorable in his entire life, and yet here he was, thinking it about his new housekeeper.

"Wash up yourself? Don't you need someone to heat the water and bring it to the bath and do all those things?" She crossed her arms over her chest and gave him a suspicious glance. "I'm not so certain you are an earl after all. You certainly don't do what normal earls do." She paused, and then her expression cleared. "Then again, you are Scottish. Perhaps that explains it."

"Yes, it must," Matthew said, wishing it were time to go back to bed rather than his just having gotten up. He was already exhausted from speaking with this woman.

And he'd have her in his immediate vicinity for an entire month.

"Thank you for meeting with me, my lord." Mr. Andrews leaned forward in his chair, his expression clearly meant to be pleasant.

Matthew did not find it so.

"My uncle tells me you have an interesting proposition." *And also wanted me to apply my rational brain to it.* Matthew found it inexplicable that the thing people found the most annoying about him—his ineffable logic—was also the thing they most relied on.

"Yes, there is a speculation opportunity that, when it works out—"

"*If* it works out," Matthew corrected.

"Yes, of course…" Mr. Andrews said. "If it works out, it will benefit not only your uncle and his family, but generations to come."

"That is a bold statement." Usually Matthew had found such hyperbole to be merely that.

"If I may, my lord," Mr. Andrews said, leaning down to open a portfolio at his feet, withdrawing a sheaf of papers from it.

Wonderful. Matthew had also found that the more hyperbolic the statements were, the more paper accompanied the pronouncement. At this rate, he would be here until dinnertime.

Which meant he would have to figure out his dinner, wouldn't he, since he'd told Miss Tyne he could fend for himself? Why had he done that, anyway?

Right. Because he didn't like having people around, fussing over him. Which meant he hadn't entirely thought it through, which meant that at this moment, it seemed like it was an idiotic decision, especially since he was hungry. Miss Tyne had made neither toast nor oatmeal, although her tea was…quite pleasant.

But he hadn't had much time this morning for such frivolity as eating a proper breakfast. He had his family depending on him, as they usually did, and food and other pleasurable things could wait.

He'd found his way to his uncle's offices easily enough, and his uncle had been delighted to see him, even though he'd been disappointed that Matthew had insisted on his own lodgings. But by now his family understood his need for quiet and privacy, although he suspected his new house-keeper would have to learn that. She'd spent the time after she returned from the shop with his tea following him around and talking, nonstop, about what she'd done the night before, what she planned to do today, and what she had hopes for on the morrow.

God help him if she somehow made it to next week. But even as he thought about it, he had to smile; she was charm-ing, guilelessly so, and he found himself almost laughing at the zeal with which she'd attacked her work.

He did appreciate that, even if he didn't see the point of her dusting all of the bedrooms, given that only the two of them were in the house. It was practical to just keep the rooms tidy that one wished to use; that is what he did in his own home, so that by now he just used his office, his library, and his bedroom, leaving the rest of the house alone.

"If I may, my lord." Mr. Andrews had finally extricated the papers it seemed he wished to show Matthew, and he was laying them out on the desk between them, smoothing each corner, which then immediately rolled up again.

"How about we view them one at a time?" Matthew asked, squelching the urge to bark at the man. Because it wasn't as though they could possibly look at all of them at the same time, so it wasn't necessary for them to be out altogether.

If only people could apply logic to situations, life, or at least Matthew's life, would be a lot easier.

"Of course. You'll see, this is the initial offering," Mr. Andrews poked a stubby finger at one of the papers, holding the corner down with his other hand. "The reasoning of the Chinese Silk Conglomerate is that we wish to bring products—"

"Silk, I presume?" Matthew interrupted.

"Yes, silk, of course. We wish to bring silk to England and other European countries, utilizing the same routes the opium boats used."

"The boats are still carrying opium, however, surely? I had not heard the trade had been suspended."

Mr. Andrews's face drew grim. "It has not, but it is only a matter of time, my lord. The conflict with China over the trade as well as our own moral obligation requires that we stop this dangerous drug from entering our country, tampering with our working class, enticing the upper classes into a life of debauchery and—"

"Yes, yes, of course," Matthew interrupted again before the man could launch into what was clearly an oft-rehearsed tirade. "You foresee the opium trade will be gone, and yet there is still a need for trade with China, and you believe silk—fabric—will substitute for an addictive drug?" He didn't work at all at keeping the skepticism from his tone.

Mr. Andrews did not seem to notice, however, but moved on to the next piece of paper.

"This shows the trade routes, with the estimates for what each ship might carry. We've calculated a percentage of loss, along with the need for repairs and other necessary expenditures. If you'll see there," he drew his finger down a long column of numbers, "you'll see each investor is still guaranteed to make a tidy sum, and that amount will increase through each successive year."

"There is no guarantee to anything, Mr. Andrews." You wouldn't think you'd have to point out such an obvious point to a businessman, but you would be wrong.

"Of course, my lord."

"And the investment amount is?"

Mr. Andrews inhaled, and Matthew knew it was going to be a very, very large number. The larger the amount, the bigger the inhale. And this was why his uncle had asked him to consult; Matthew had the ability to review any number of business plans and ventures and decide, usually on the spot, if they were worth the risk.

Mr. Andrews pointed at a third piece of paper, spreading it out to reveal the enormous sum required.

Even Matthew was startled, and he did not startle easily. If Mr. Andrews were correct and the trade took off, the family would have their fortunes made. But if not, it would well ruin his uncle's bank and would likely take down several branches of the family.

Since Matthew never invested in anything he'd advised someone else on, it wouldn't matter to him one way or the other, financially. But it would matter to him as it affected his family; many of them lacked the most basic common sense, but he cared for them, all of them, and he did not wish to see them ruined. Particularly not his uncle, who'd raised him after Matthew's father had died.

"Silk? Why silk?" Matthew asked.

Mr. Andrews glanced at Matthew's hand. "You are not married, my lord?"

"No." He hadn't found the appropriate woman yet, but he planned on doing just that when he returned home. A woman who would be a good mother to his children, who would be quiet and understanding and who would not demand too much of him.

"Sisters?" Mr. Andrews continued. It seemed the man would not stop prying until Matthew admitted to having some females in his life.

"Yes, sisters." Four of them, all of whom were younger, sillier, and, he had to admit, more joyful than he. Two of the sisters were already married, but he had yet to get the final two taken care of. A wife would be able to assist there, as well.

"Then you know young ladies do love to wear pretty gowns," Mr. Andrews said in a triumphant tone of voice. "And there's nothing prettier than Chinese silk, I assure you. Let me show you," he began, reaching into his bag of unending papers and now, it seemed, fabric samples as well.

"Certainly, Mr. Andrews, if you would just leave everything with me, I will sit down with your papers and…and your materials, and review."

"My partners and I will require a decision from your uncle within two weeks. We have other investors willing to come aboard, but I wanted to give MacIntyre and Sons the first opportunity. The ships will be leaving by March."

"Of course," Matthew said. It was an old trick, pressing the investor for a decision within a certain time frame. In this case it suited his purposes, since he did not wish to be in London for any longer than his allotted month.

"Thank you for your time, my lord," Mr. Andrews said, getting up from his chair to dump many scraps of fabric on Matthew's desk.

"Thank you," Matthew said dryly as he eyed the mess.

"Well?" Uncle Jonas's voice had an anxious note, as though he were dreading Matthew's judgment. Matthew wondered which judgment he was hoping for, or whether it was more of an open-ended anxiety; after all, if Matthew advised against investing, and the investment turned out to be a solid one, his uncle would not benefit. On the other hand, if he did advise for it, and it did not work out, then Uncle Jonas would be jeopardizing his family's, as well as perhaps his bank's, future.

Matthew did not envy his uncle those kinds of decisions. That was why he had taken on the role of advisor. His title came with a manor estate, a house in Edinburgh, and acres that he leased to various farmers. He was not incredibly wealthy, but he had everything suitable for his needs. He didn't see the point of trying to increase his fortune; it wasn't as though he could possibly spend everything he had now, and his investments and holdings were solid enough to ensure his children, when he found the woman to bear them, of course. Which, according to his plans, would be sometime within the next six months.

"I can't just decide based on one meeting, Uncle," Matthew said in as kind a voice as he could manage. Judging by how his uncle winced, it wasn't all that kind. "I need time to review the papers"—*all of them, so help me*—"and review the goals of the corporation and do all the required research. That is why I committed to spending a month here, Uncle, not just a few days."

"Of course, my boy. Thank you for making the trip. I hope the house and your temporary staff is up to your standards. You know you may come stay with us." His uncle leaned in closer, a conspiratorial note to his voice. "There is a young lady, a distant relation, who is staying with us for a few months. She is quite a suitable woman, unmarried, and she will make a fine wife for a man such as yourself." Uncle Jonas folded his arms over his chest. "And in just a few weeks it will be Valentine's Day, and what better way to celebrate than with a charming young woman who would make an even more charming bride?"

Matthew gave a tight smile in return. He'd shared his plans with his uncle in their correspondence, laying out his plans for the next few years of his life, so it wasn't unexpected that his uncle would be trying to find him a bride. But for some reason, reasons he didn't want to explore; it didn't sit right, not at this time, at least.

Plus Valentine's Day was a ridiculous holiday, one that he did his best to ignore. He did not wish to be prancing around some lady who was hoping for flowers or poetry or some other nonsense that he despised.

He wished that he could find some young lady who would prefer to have a book, so at least they'd have something in common. But he hadn't yet, and it didn't seem likely, so he would likely just have to settle.

It was very good his uncle had no clue what he was thinking. Instead, Uncle Jonas's expression seemed to indicate that he thought he was offering the treat of the century.

"You should come dine with us tonight, in fact. I presume you have not made other plans?"

He hadn't. Not even for toast or oatmeal.

"Of course. I will just go home and change, and then return at—?"

His uncle beamed.

"Seven o'clock. And you may meet Miss Delaney; she is a lovely girl. And there is plenty of room, if you want to stay with us, as I said. The house is very comfortable, surely better than whatever you've rented."

Matthew thought about the warmth of the bed, the way his housekeeper seemed absolutely delighted to share her lack of cooking skills with him, how her eyes had sparkled when she was persuading him to at least have tea, and how the light streamed through the windows after she'd raised the curtains.

Funny, he didn't always remember to raise the curtains in his own rooms at home. He would have to bear in mind that for some reason it lifted his spirits, irrational though that seemed.

"Thank you," Matthew replied. "I will see you at seven."

A Belle's Guide to Household Management

A housekeeper is always addressed as "Mrs.," perhaps because her only marital expectations are to be married to the house.

CHAPTER FIVE

"Watch your feet as you come in, I've just mopped." Matthew halted as he drew the key from the door, then leapt to where he could see a dry spot on the hallway floor, feeling like an idiot. Or a frog. Or both.

She appeared at the end of the hallway, the soft twilight framing her as though she were in a painting.

"Good evening, my lord." She hopped from dry spot to dry spot, eventually landing on the nearest spot to him. Very near; he could see faint freckles on her cheeks and a smudge on her nose.

Before he even thought about it, he raised his hand to her face and swiped the smudge off, nearly smiling at her startled expression. Nearly.

"Good evening, Miss Tyne." This close, he could smell the faint fragrance of lemon, perhaps the cleaning solution she'd been using. And there was something else, too, something rather feminine and warm and soft.

Or that was just her.

"I'm home just to change my clothes. I am going to my uncle's for dinner." *Where I will meet an entirely suitable young lady, one who probably doesn't have freckles and smells of some-thing floral and delicate, not warmth and lemons and softness.*

And wasn't that a fanciful thought for him to have? *What would softness smell like, anyway?* Before he knew it, he found himself sniffing.

"Do you have a cold? I will just go make you some tea; you need something in case you are coming down with some-thing," she said, a concerned look on her face. "I took the liberty of putting your clothing away, and it appears you need a fresh cravat. I will just iron it while you have tea."

Matthew normally did not allow anyone to order him about, but soon he found himself seated in the kitchen, a cup of tea and a piece of burnt toast at his elbow, Miss Tyne busily ironing his cravat in front of the stove.

"And how were your meetings, my lord?" she asked, her tone sounding as though she were actually interested. She didn't wait for his reply before continuing. "My day was spent in meetings with dust and grime. I am surprised the rental agent allowed the house to be let like this. I cleaned your bed-room, so it is all ready for you this evening. I hope it is to your liking; the sheets and room are clean, at least."

Matthew took a sip of the tea. Made just how he liked it, and he'd only told her once how he took it. That warmed him as much as the tea did.

"If it is a bed, it will suit me fine," he said, feeling for the first time how his travel and uncomfortable sleeping position last night had affected him. He wished he didn't have to go out to his uncle's tonight; he wanted to stay here. Specifically, stay here with her and her charming manner, and how she asked questions she really wanted to know the answers to but didn't wait for a reply, since it seemed her mind was traveling so quickly.

He hadn't met many ladies who weren't entirely circumspect in their speech before. He found it oddly refreshing.

"And your meetings?" she asked again, her head still bent to her task.

"Fine." There was so much to research; he knew it could be done within a few weeks, but so much was riding on his decision: not only his uncle's money, but the livelihood of the people he employed, not to mention Mr. Andrews's employees and the people who manufactured the fabric Mr. Andrews wished to sell.

He felt an unfamiliar exhaustion creeping over him, not just from his general fatigue but with always having to be responsible for so many people. His mother and his sisters, his workers, his tenants, more distant family like his uncle and others, and all the people who knew him to be responsible and thoughtful, so would come asking for his advice.

Nobody but her had ever asked, with any sincerity, how he was feeling.

The earl let out one of those long-suffering sighs with which Annabelle was familiar; normally it was when people had spoken with her for more than ten minutes or so, but his expression was distant, not as though he were thinking of her at all. Which piqued her, but was also satisfying; she didn't want him to be another person who was annoyed or irritated at having to speak with her.

She knew full well that she could be both annoying and irritating. She'd tried to be circumspect, to behave as all those polite young ladies did. But whenever she tried, she felt as though something were being smothered inside of herself, and then she blurted out something worse than she would have if she had just been being herself.

Maybe she should teach the How to Speak to Annabelle class, because then she could just say, "I am who I am, and I am fine being that way, thank you."

It would be a very short class, and likely not worth anyone's time or money.

"What is it?" she asked, setting the iron up on the surface she'd been ironing on and casting a critical gaze on the cravat. It was fine, but she wanted to prolong their time together, so she laid it out as though she had spotted a wrinkle and began to work again.

A pause, and she wondered if he was going to reply or just sit there and sigh, not deeming his mere housekeeper worthy of a reply.

"There's a lady I am going to meet this evening."

Why did that make her stomach tighten? Oh, of course, because he was an attractive man, and she'd just met him, not to mention they'd very briefly shared a bed. But he was an earl, even if it was a Scottish title, whereas she, she was just Annabelle, partner in the Quality Employment Agency and a surrogate housekeeper.

"I know my uncle means well. I'm just…I hadn't planned on it." He sounded genuinely perturbed, and she had the sense that surprises were generally not allowed to happen to him. No wonder he'd been so startled at finding her in the house when he hadn't expected her until the following day. "I know I will wed, it is my right and my duty, but I came here with one purpose, not two."

"What about love?" She couldn't help the words that spilled out of her, any more than she could help how her stomach tightened even more at the thought of marrying just for right and duty. "Love is the reason"—*sometimes the only reason*, she thought—"so many of us do things. They may not always be the right things, but they are the things that matter. Love matters." She felt the burn of unshed tears and chided herself for being so emotional, especially in front of this man to whom emotion seemed like another annoyance.

"I wish I felt as you do, Miss Tyne," he answered. His tone wasn't condemning, but wistful. As though he really did wish he felt that way.

It had been a while since anybody had taken her seriously. And she didn't think a man ever had. Long ago, before she'd known people could be deceptive, she'd thought a man had. And she'd fallen for him, fallen in love, and become a fallen woman.

And he'd let her lie there rather than help her up. Other women might have turned their back on love permanently, but not Annabelle; she'd known men like Charles were out there and might try to take advantage of her again, but she wouldn't forswear love just because of a few deceptive men. She'd try to be wise in whom she admired, would try to remember, since she was incapable of lying herself, that others would lie in pursuit of their goals.

And she had to admit that even though she had fallen, as she had so thoroughly after Charles, at least it had brought her the agency and her friends.

Besides which, all the books she read seemed to indicate that having some sort of horrible thing happen to someone then resulted in a wonderful thing happening. She was hoping it wasn't just fiction.

"You can feel as I do, my lord," she said softly. He shook his head "no" almost as soon as the words were out of her mouth.

"You have to open your heart to the possibilities." She began to fold the cravat. "Perhaps this lady you will meet tonight, perhaps she is the one you are destined to love."

"I don't believe in destiny," he said, his voice scornful. "Destiny is what people blame when their own foolishness caused a mishap in their lives. Destiny, fate, what God intended; it's all an excuse for people who aren't strong enough to control their own lives."

Her heart hurt at how harsh and bitter he sounded. "Some people do that, yes. But I didn't meant destiny as though you can't do anything to control it yourself. I mean it as something you have to be open to. Not something you control, or don't control. Just…your future. Whatever it might be, you have to be open to making choices."

"Risk-taking is for fools who can't predict the future, Miss Tyne." He lifted his gaze to regard her face, his expression looking almost chagrined. "Although I don't suppose you are a fool, I apologize if it seems as though I called you one."

Annabelle shook her head ruefully. "You are not the first person to have called me a fool, even if you didn't mean it, and you will not be the last. I learned a long time ago that what is right for me is not right for others. I do so hope that happiness is right for you, my lord."

Long after he'd changed his clothing and put on his freshly ironed cravat, long after he'd exchanged pleasantries with the very pleasant young lady his uncle had introduced him to, even after he'd made his final good-byes and was making his way back home in a creaky carriage, her words echoed in his head: "I do so hope that happiness is right for you."

He leaned back against the carriage seat and gazed out the window. It was night, but there were a few lamps lit against the bleak darkness, and here and there Matthew saw movement in the shadows. Did those people have happiness in their future? What made him so deserving?

The only thing that seemed to matter was his ability to decide things for other people. And that he had been born to his particular father in a particular region, and thus had inherited particular holdings.

Could that bring him happiness? Suddenly, the thought of what happiness could be rushed in on him so quickly he started. A woman, a woman with a quick laugh, a ready wit, and an ability to laugh at herself and at him, waiting for him when he returned home. A woman who would, perhaps, upset his orderly way of life, but not for the worst, as he'd always imagined. Maybe for the better, even though he'd never thought of that possibility before.

The carriage pulled up in front of the house and he descended, pressing a few coins into the hackney driver's hand. By now he was accustomed to the man's making a comment about his country of origin, and he waved his hand in dismissal as he ascended the stairs.

Long after he had washed and changed, long after he'd found his now-clean bedroom and crawled into bed, long after he'd watched the clock move from twelve o'clock to one o'clock to two o'clock, he heard her voice.

"I do so hope that happiness is right for you."

A Belle's Guide to Household Management

We wish to encourage everyone, not just housekeepers, to refrain from biting the dust. Either you will expire, or you will have a mouthful of unpleasantness. Either way, it is not to be desired.

Chapter Six

The week passed about the same way each day; Annabelle made tea for the earl, who spoke very little but looked at her frequently, and then he'd head off to do his work and she'd be left on her own. She'd had enough free time to work at the agency for a few hours here and there, but she was beginning to realize she needed to start the How to Speak to Annabelle class if only to hear another voice that wasn't her own speaking.

He took most meals at his uncle's house where, she presumed—but didn't want to imagine—he met many ladies who were ladies, whereas not only was she not a lady, she was also not a housekeeper. Although she had to admit she was keeping the house perfectly well, at least as much as he allowed her to.

He returned late at night, holding various amounts of paperwork and speaking just as little as he had in the morning. And yet, she got the feeling he was acutely aware of her, just as she was acutely aware of him.

There was a substantial amount of acuity in the house.

On the eighth day, she heard the key turn in the door earlier than was his custom. She'd still spent the past five hours completely on her own, and she'd been reduced to speaking with the mice she assumed were present but couldn't see.

Heaven help her if she did see them, since she was terrified of mice. And don't even speak about rats.

She'd read some of her book, but it was so oddly distracting to be alone in this big house, so quiet, where she was accustomed to the noise of the other tenants in her building, the comings and goings of all the other workers who lived there. She didn't know if she'd ever get accustomed to the quiet, especially after only a week.

He'd been very late the night before; she hadn't heard him come in, but then again she'd been completely exhausted from her day of cleaning and had eaten a quick dinner (oatmeal, no toast) and then taken herself off to bed, alone, long before she even expected him to arrive.

That morning, as usual, she'd caught him staring at her a few times, as though he wished to ask something, but wasn't certain.

Hopefully it wasn't anything about why the toast was always burnt, because she simply did not have an answer. It just was. Was that the toast's destiny? She wished she could point out the joke to him, but she was thinking he might not find it nearly as amusing as she did.

"Good evening, my lord," she said, shutting the book and placing it on the table beside her. She rose and walked to where the earl stood, smoothing her not-quite-worst dress. "I trust you had a pleasant day? Let me have that," she said, taking the large case he was carrying without waiting for him to reply. Or even to hand it over, judging by how his grip had tightened as she drew it away.

"Good evening, Miss Tyne," the earl replied, his eyes on where she held the case.

"You look tired. Are you tired? That is, I know it is rude to comment on how someone looks, at least unless the someone has a piece of food in their teeth, in which case it would be rude not to point it out, for fear that the person might be embarrassed later on. What if the Queen should happen to stop by?"

The earl gaped at her as though she were speaking a foreign language, an impossibility since she didn't know any.

"The Queen is not likely to stop by, as you say, Miss Tyne." The earl sounded tired as well. It appeared she would have to supply his end of the conversation as well that evening. "Miss Tyne," he continued, before she could announce her plans for monologuing, "I am hungry, and I would like it if you would accompany me for some dinner. I presume you have not eaten? I do not recall you buying either bread or oatmeal," he said in a nearly humorous tone.

Was he actually making a joke? The Earl of Dour?

"I would love to, my lord," she said, responding without even thinking about the impropriety of her employer, a member of the aristocracy, taking his employee, a fallen woman who was attempting to right herself, out for a meal.

Well, or not thinking about it very much. Or about the fact that he wasn't at his uncle's, for once, but was home with apparently no plans but to take her out somewhere. And since she was hungry and he seemed to want company, and if all he needed was for her to be present and answer the door and tidy his things, it didn't seem like too much to ask for her to accompany him to dine. Besides which, she was tired of talking to the mice. They hadn't read her book, after all, so they had little to discuss with one another.

"Shall we?" the earl said, pulling her cloak down from the peg by the door. He held it out for her, and she slid her arms in, very aware of how close he was, and how much power he seemed to exude, not to mention how incredibly handsome he was.

She wondered if he knew just how handsome he was. Perhaps she wouldn't ask him, at least not this evening when they had just barely met.

"Do you know where we should go?" she asked instead, a much more innocuous question, and definitely more pertinent, than inquiring if he'd ever noticed his own looks.

"I saw a tavern a few streets away. It looked suitable," he replied, as she buttoned her cloak and pulled the hood over her head.

"Excellent," Annabelle said, as he opened the door, that deliciously lovely feeling of being in the presence of aristocracy curling in her stomach.

Although if she were honest with herself, which she always was, she would have to say it was mostly because of the aforementioned handsomeness, because he was a Scottish earl, and those didn't seem to count as much. Although, since he was the only Scot and the only earl she'd ever known, perhaps she should say Scottish earls—the ones in her acquaintance, at least—mattered quite a lot.

The tavern was nearby, and Annabelle was relieved to see other women inside, not that she wouldn't have gone in anyway, but at least it seemed somewhat more proper for her to be there if there were other women there, too. None of the other women were ladies, but then again, none of the men in there were gentlemen, either, so it seemed proper enough.

The earl, Scottish though he was, was the only gentleman within, in fact.

He ensured she was properly settled, then sat himself opposite her at a low table in the back. He exhaled, one of those long, "I've just been speaking to Annabelle too long" sighs, only they hadn't spoken at all.

So that would be up to her. "How was your day, my lord?" she asked.

He shook his head. "I don't want to talk about it."

She felt as though he'd rebuffed her and felt momentarily hurt, until he met her gaze. "Tell me about yours. What were you reading when I came home?" And now it sounded as though he was really interested, and didn't that make her feel all sparkly and alive.

Not that sitting in a tavern with the most attractive man she'd ever seen—and an earl—wasn't sparkle-inducing enough.

"Do you read, my lord?" She didn't wait for his reply. "Because I do, I mean I can read, of course, but I also love to read. And not just recipes, which as you likely know already, I don't read at all, but books. I was reading Mr. Dickens's *The Pickwick Papers*; it is one of my favorites."

His face looked as though it was about to break into a smile, and she held her breath waiting for it.

Drat. No smile, but at least his tone was warm. "I enjoy Mr. Dickens as well. I find reading to be a welcome relief after working all day."

Annabelle wrinkled her brow. "I didn't realize earls did work, I mean, beyond being all *earl-y*," she said, hoping this time that he would get the joke or at least acknowledge it.

He did smile then, and she felt as though fire from the tavern's fireplace had just leapt out and enveloped her in its warmth. "Perhaps they don't, but I do. I like working, I like being…useful." The way he said it made it sound as though he was embarrassed about it.

"I like to work as well. I can't imagine not working. I mean, I would enjoy a week or so of sitting at home and just reading, but I think I would go mad with boredom."

He nodded, as though he agreed—again!—and now she felt practically on fire herself, she was so warm.

She opened her mouth to continue, but stopped when she heard another voice.

"Be right there," the barmaid called. "Two pints?" she asked, nodding toward them, and the earl nodded. But the interruption seemed to make him realize he'd been speaking and even smiling, since his whole self returned to his more somber mien.

At least she no longer felt as though she might spontaneously combust. Even if she did miss his smile.

"And the young lady you met at your uncle's house one of those first evenings. Was she nice?" Miss Tyne's voice was more subdued than usual, the question sounding as though she wasn't certain she wished to hear the answer. Unlike all the other questions she'd asked thus far.

He'd felt, for just a few moments, what it would be like to speak with someone when they had things in common, and not just about an investment opportunity. He wanted to find out what other books she liked, if they shared more than Mr. Dickens in their taste. But she was waiting for his answer, not for more questions. Not that he'd even know how to ask the questions; he wasn't accustomed to speaking to anyone of common interests.

Matthew thought of Miss Delaney. She was perfectly pleasant, lowering her eyes in shyness or politeness, he wasn't sure. Not that it mattered. He'd found himself comparing her with his housekeeper, and Miss Delaney, to his surprise, had been found wanting. And it wasn't for lack of opportunity; he'd deliberately taken his dinners at his uncle's house, and Miss Delaney was staying there, so he had gotten to know her, somewhat. But he doubted whether she could ever compare.

He shrugged. "She was very pleasant. She finds the weather tolerable and likes to visit the National Gallery, and she plays the pianoforte. Oh, thank you," Matthew said to the barmaid who brought two pints of ale. "I'll have the beef pie, and the lady will have—?"

Miss Tyne smiled up at the barmaid so brightly it nearly hurt Matthew's eyes. "The beef pie sounds wonderful. Is it good? Do you recommend it?"

Here she was, again asking questions as though she really wished to hear the answer. The barmaid's expression blossomed like an opening flower.

"It is, miss, it is the cook's special recipe. And the pies were just made today. Sometimes Cook doesn't get a chance to make them, so we've got the day before's, only they aren't quite as good. These are lovely."

Was it possible for Miss Tyne to smile even more broadly? Apparently so.

"That is what I will have, then. Thank you so much."

The barmaid nodded, still smiling, then walked away from their table.

Matthew leaned forward to her. "How do you do that?"

"Do what?" she said, glancing around as though she'd done something.

"Make everyone you're speaking to feel as though they're the only person in the world you wish to speak to."

She blinked in surprise. "But it is the truth. I don't try to be anything I'm not," at which point she colored up, "and I do like to speak to people. All sorts of people. Barmaids and hackney drivers and even, on occasion, gruff earls from Scotland who surprise me when I'm sleeping." She grinned and took a sip of her ale.

Matthew felt himself start to blush also, remembering the moment—*was it just a week or so before?*—that he'd gotten into that bed with her. It had seemed shocking at the time, of course, but now that he'd seen her and spent time in her company, it also seemed as though it were something he wished would happen again.

Even though that thought was entirely unlike him. He was not spontaneous, he was not particularly lustful, and he seldom entertained inappropriate thoughts.

And yet here he was, doing all three. And while he could have blamed it on being in London, a city he'd never been in before, he had to acknowledge that it was most likely Annabelle who was making him feeling this way.

And he wasn't sure how he felt. About any of it, and that uncertainty was perhaps the most unlike him thing he'd ever felt.

Thankfully, their food arrived before he could ponder his own anomalies any further.

"What is Scotland like? I've never been, at least not that I know of." Miss Tyne rested her elbows on the wooden table, her eyes the brightest spark in the dimly lit pub.

Conversation had stopped when the food arrived. Both he and Miss Tyne were apparently starving, since they spent the first fifteen minutes of their meal together in complete silence, both just concentrating on eating.

He'd glanced at her a few times, of course, just to ensure they weren't in some sort of awkward silence of which he wasn't aware, but she seemed just as happy as he was not to talk. That was unexpected, given how much she seemed to like to talk. Unexpected, but not one of those unpleasant unexpected surprises; instead, it felt as though he might not know all about her yet. That was unusual as well; normally he could assess a person within a few minutes of making their acquaintance.

"It's like here, I suppose."

"Here like a pub, filled with laborers and solicitors and men who seem as though they are very important? Possibly a few women who appreciate the company of important men?" Her smirk told him she was joking. That she saw fit to do so was another unexpected item to add to the list of things he now knew about her. Few people joked with him, and of those, he liked very few of their jokes.

What made her so different from most people?

"No, Miss Literal, not like here." He allowed himself to roll his eyes at her. Something he normally chided his sisters for doing. Of course, they were usually rolling their eyes at him. "Where I live, in town, Edinburgh that is, is a busy city much like London. Different accents, of course, but most things are the same."

Now it was her turn to roll her eyes. "Honestly, the same? I should think not, and I've never even been there! The people, the language, the food, the habits, the celebrations, the clothes—all of those things are different in different areas. The west side of London is different from the docks, correct? You wouldn't say all of London is all the same; how can you say Edinburgh is?"

She waved her hand around the pub. "Even here, where things are the same, the people are different. You, for example, are clearly of the nobility; your linen is fresh, your clothing is well-kept and well-made, and you are well-groomed." She picked his hand up from the table and examined his fingers. "Your nails are cut, and you don't even have any dirt underneath your fingernails."

He drew his hand back and looked at it. She was correct, and he hadn't even thought about it.

"Now look at my hand," she said, stretching it out to him. He took it, the warmth of her skin reminding him of before when his naked body had been close to hers, however briefly.

He could not get distracted by that, however. It wasn't practical.

Her hand was small and its shape was delicate, but the skin was rough and her fingernails were ragged, although clean. He looked at the back of her hand, then turned her hand over and looked at her palm, which had a few red spots where calluses were beginning to form.

"You're not a housekeeper," he said, sliding the pad of his finger along one of those new calluses. "If you were accustomed to this sort of work, your hands would be rougher. You obviously work with your hands in some capacity, but not doing what you did today."

"Oh!" she said, snatching her hand back and stuffing them into her pockets. "You are very observant, even if you think two completely different cities are similar to one another." She stuck her tongue out at him quickly, then clapped her hand over her mouth, her eyes wide. "I am so sorry, I should not have done that."

Matthew tried to keep himself from smiling, but couldn't, not in the face of such…joy. She was practically overflowing with it, and he wished he could figure out a way to capture some of that joy for himself. "I am not offended at all; in fact my sisters would be applauding you right now." He spoke in a lower tone. "I am very glad they are not here for that very reason." Not to mention he was definitely liking being alone with her, and wasn't that another surprise?

"Shall we go?" Matthew said, signaling to the man behind the bar. He made the "final bill" gesture, then drew out a few coins from his pocket and laid them on the table.

The barkeep came bustling over, an obsequious smile on his face. "Four shillings, my lord."

Matthew counted out the four shillings, then rose from his seat.

The barkeep picked up the coins, scowling. "You're Scottish, aren't you?" he said in an accusing tone.

Why did that keep coming up?

Matthew didn't bother to reply, just strode around to Miss Tyne's side of the table and took her cloak, holding it up so she could put it on.

As she wriggled into it, her arm brushed his side, and Matthew felt something very unexpected indeed.

Something he wished to expect more of, and hopefully in the near future.

A Belle's Guide to Household Management

When asked to put Holland covers on the furniture to protect it while the members of the household are away, do not assume that you may only use covers made in Holland or that the covers are meant to cover the country in question.

CHAPTER SEVEN

Annabelle preceded him from the pub, the happy warmth of the food they'd eaten warring with the uneasy feeling that he was about to ask her why she was his housekeeper if she wasn't a housekeeper at all.

"Are you going to tell me?" he asked in a conspiratorial tone as he drew alongside her.

"Tell you what?" she replied, even though she knew perfectly well what it was, and she was just stalling.

He chuckled, and she realized she hadn't heard him laugh yet. Not that they'd been acquainted all that long, but generally, if the people she met were friendly and relatively conversational, she was able to make them at least laugh a little bit. Him, not a whit. He had smiled, and had almost smiled a few times more than that, and he had definitely made a witty remark, but he hadn't laughed.

She liked the sound of it. A lot. She wanted him to laugh more. For her.

"Tell me what you are if you are not a housekeeper."

Annabelle tilted her head up to look at him. "I am also not a lion tamer. Despite how ferocious you might seem." That surprised a quick smile from him. And encouraged her to continue. "I am also not a princess, a haberdasher, a scullery maid, a cook."

"Obviously," he interjected.

"A butcher, a carriage driver, a…let me see, what else am I not?"

She hadn't noticed, but somehow she'd taken his arm, and was leaning on it as they walked. It felt so comfortable and yet also caused a tingling sensation throughout her entire body.

"Perhaps you are the Queen?" He drew away and gave her an appraising look. "No, you are far too frivolous. Although if you had food in your teeth it wouldn't matter because it would be you who would possibly be bothered by it." He frowned, as though in confusion. "Now I am using your logic." He shook his head. "Only a few hours in your presence, Miss Tyne, and I am overwhelmed."

Was that a compliment?

"The only thing I do know, Miss Tyne, is that you are not a housekeeper. Tell me. Are you also not a Miss? Is there a Mr. Tyne somewhere, perhaps a brood of small Tynes running about?" There was a sharp edge to his voice that hadn't been there before. Interesting.

Annabelle wasn't naive; she knew the earl found her attractive, perhaps even intriguing, overwhelming, and she felt a surge of satisfaction at the confirmation. And since he was only here for a few weeks more and he was from Scotland of all places, never mind he was an earl as well, it didn't matter. Except to her sense of vanity, which was quite pleased.

"No, I am just me. Miss Tyne, nonhousekeeper. Partial owner of the Quality Employment Agency, and your representative demanded someone immediately."

"Ah, I was wondering what had happened. My uncle promised to find someone quickly." He thought for a moment. "So you are part owner of the agency, the one that hired you out?" He shook his head, feeling entirely confused. Or what it must be like to be inside her head. "How does that work? Do you pay a percentage of your fee to yourself?"

She nudged him and laughed. "You're funny, do you know that?"

Actually, he didn't. No one had ever accused him of being funny before. Unless it was funny odd, like when his business contacts invited him to a brothel and he'd said no, he'd prefer to go home and read.

Now he'd have to say he'd prefer to go home and read with her. Sitting in chairs next to a fireplace, tea made just as they each liked it at their elbows, perhaps a stray feline wandering through, although that thought was even more funny, given that he had never given much of a thought to cats or where they might like to wander.

She shrugged before he could respond. Because of course he hadn't responded, his mind had just wandered off, catlike, into a world where they were equals, enjoying each other's company and where it didn't matter whether or not she was a housekeeper—not that she was—or that he was an earl.

"I do promise, my lord, that even though I am not what you hired me as, I will do all the work necessary to fulfill my function as your housekeeper as you've laid the work out for me..."—she still had hold of his arm, but she held her palm up and ticked off the tasks with her free hand—"answering the door, keeping things tidy, making the tea, not to mention doing all—"

But her words were lost when he suddenly turned, walked her against the wall of a building they were passing, and pressed his lips to hers.

And he knew that right then, right at this moment, it didn't matter who they were. They were man and woman, male and female, gentleman and lady. And it felt absolutely, perfectly right.

Annabelle had been kissed before—and more, she wasn't a fallen woman just because she'd lost her footing—but never so suddenly, so solidly, or so unexpectedly.

Her back was against the cold stone of the building, and her front—well, her front was pressed against the warm hardness of him, as solid as the stone at her back but much more welcome.

And then, just when she was exclaiming delightedly in her head about this turn of events, it was over.

He drew back, his eyes searching hers, his hands holding her elbows as though to steady her, even though she was not in danger of falling. Not literally falling, at least.

"I am so sorry, Miss Tyne. I did not, I do not, know what came over..." he began, his gorgeous mouth forming words she didn't want to hear.

"Hush," she said, sliding her palms over his forearms, up his biceps, then curling her fingers in his hair and drawing his mouth…yes, that same gorgeous mouth…back to hers. "Kiss me."

Matthew could count on one hand the number of times he'd acted impulsively. One finger would suffice, and that was only because he had begun to kiss her just now. Previously, his count would have taken no hands.

And it would have been just a kiss, one simple pressing of mouths together in a brief moment of impulsiveness if she hadn't wanted more, if she hadn't pulled him back to her and twined her hands in his hair so he couldn't escape, even if he wanted to.

He did not want to. He leaned into her, slanted his mouth over hers, put his hands at her waist and held her, then opened his mouth just a bit so as to coax hers to open as well. Her lips were warm and moist, and their bodies touched just at the most delicious places—her breasts, his cock, their mouths. A perfect triumvirate of passion that was unlike anything he'd ever experienced before. And he had indulged before, just not to completion, so he did have some perspective on the matter.

She did take the hint, and she opened to him, sliding her tongue into his mouth and uttering a soft moan low, deep in her throat, that sent an answering shiver through him.

And they were both still entirely clothed, out on the street, where anyone—

"We have to stop," he said, pulling away from her mouth but not yet strong enough to lift his hands from her waist. Her expression was dazed, and he felt a brief moment of triumph that he, as little experienced in such things as he was, could reduce her to that state with just a simple kiss.

But it wasn't simple, not at all, not when you thought of the touching of bodies and mouths, the tangling of tongues, the soft sigh that had escaped her, the way his cock had reacted to the feel of her body against his.

Not simple at all.

"I apologize," Matthew said stiffly as he drew away from her mouth and her warm, luscious form.

"Oh hush, my lord," she replied, as though it was customary for her to be kissed on London streets. And perhaps it was; what did he know about her, except that she was not a housekeeper? But he also knew there wasn't a deceptive bone in her body, just a joyful frankness that was unlike anything he'd ever encountered before. So the fact that it seemed as though she was not upset or prudish about what had happened was as natural to her as it would have been for another lady to slap his face for his familiarity. Even if the latter lady had secretly enjoyed it.

He far preferred her response.

"If I hadn't wanted you to kiss me, I wouldn't have engaged you in a kiss. Isn't that your logic? 'If I had wanted a cook, I would have hired one,'" she said, lowering her voice and trying for a Scottish accent, which she mangled very badly.

He felt his lips curl up into a tight grimace, as though discussing the aftereffects of an impetuous kiss on a London street was something he could smile about. It was not, not at all, and a part of him, the part of him that was making its presence quite well-known in his trousers, wished he would just push her up against the building again and ravage her mouth, taste her sweet lips, and run his palms all over her curves. Better yet, take her home where there was a place where they might get horizontal with one another and not have to risk being seen.

Home. Hell, that was where they were both going, wasn't it? Not that the London house was his home, per se, but it was acting in place of his home for the duration. The month he was in town sorting out his uncle's business, being seen off and welcomed home every day…and night…by this woman whom he already found intoxicating.

He would have to maintain his renowned attributes of propriety and sense in keeping himself away from her.

He already hated that far, far more than either being early, being late, or wasting money.

It seemed she made him lose his speech, and perhaps part of his brain, judging by the expression on his face. Annabelle shouldn't have been so delighted by this turn of events—the kiss and his reaction to it—as much as she was, but the truth was, she was, and she was curious, so curious, about how she could get under his skin, not to mention onto his mouth.

Being a fallen woman had its benefits; she knew precisely what she could do to keep herself from being permanently fallen, and she also wasn't scared, as so many other young unmarried ladies were, of what men wanted and what they frequently wanted to do with young unmarried ladies.

Of course she wouldn't take advantage of him, and then had to remind herself not to smirk at the thought. He would think she was laughing at him, when really she was just amused by the thought that she could possibly be in power over an earl, even if he was Scottish.

"Shall we walk?" she said instead, pushing herself off the wall and onto her own two, admittedly unsteady, feet.

He nodded and held his arm out for her, as stiffly as he'd spoken earlier, and she wanted to roll her eyes and stick her tongue out at him for being so pokerish, but she didn't think he would appreciate her levity. Not, she thought, when he was so obviously perturbed by the whole thing.

"I need to ask your opinion on something," he said. His voice was low and rumbly and made Annabelle's stomach do an unexpected leap. Even though she already knew he wasn't going to ask her opinion on kissing, or anything of the sort.

More's the pity.

"Of course, my lord," she said, grasping his arm a little tighter. Goodness, he was strong. Maybe he did do his own housework; bringing in firewood, beating rugs, moving furniture around, and other tasks would certainly build up his muscles. Perhaps there were different requirements for earls of the Scottish persuasion, so it was necessary for them to be all muscular as well as handsome.

Or maybe it was only this one. In which case she was quite pleased she had not ended up with, say, the gouty earl with the high-pitched cackle and a penchant for eating smelly fish.

Not that she knew if this one ate smelly fish, but she knew about the rest of it.

"My uncle has asked me to town to consult on an investment he is considering, ah, investing in." He sounded irked at having to repeat a word, and Annabelle hoped it was because she had loosened his brain with her kiss. Or something like that.

"And it is something about which I know very little, and I would like your thoughts about it."

Was it a manual on how to remain cheerful despite all of life's problems? Or maybe he was the one teaching the How to Speak to Annabelle class, and he thought he'd come to the source. It couldn't be her toast or oatmeal skills, those were minimal, and he'd only had her tea thus far. It couldn't be How to Make Tea, unless he was a complete idiot.

Which he wasn't. He'd kissed her, hadn't he? Right when she might have almost secretly been thinking about that very thing? Was he a mind reader?

No, because then they'd still be back there, his mouth on hers, since that was precisely what was on her mind.

"If it's not how to pretend to be a housekeeper, I'm not sure I can help you," she said, hoping he would laugh rather than glower at her.

He did both, which was better than merely glowering, but not as good as just laughing. And his face looked so funny, all screwed up in disapproval even as he was chuckling, that she had to laugh, too, at which point he forgot all about the laughing part and just glowered.

Reminder to herself: *Don't laugh at him.*

"It is for a fabric importer, and I know nothing about fabrics."

"And I do?" she said, drawing back to regard him with a puzzled look.

He sighed, as though exasperated, a response Annabelle was quite accustomed to. Maybe he had taken the class on

How to Speak to Annabelle, or its companion class, How to Respond to Annabelle in a Way that Conveyed Disappointment and Frustration.

Many, many people seemed to have taken that particular course.

And look at her, getting all mopey. She shouldn't be, not when she'd just been kissed and was walking on the arm of the most handsome man she'd ever seen, much less kissed.

Although the thought occurred to her that this man was so much more than his looks, and she wasn't certain she would ever find his equal again. That was mope-inducing, to be sure. Because no matter how Scottish earls were different from their British counterparts, she knew neither type would ever get involved more permanently with a not-housekeeper who was also a not-aristocrat.

"You know what ladies appreciate in clothing, I presume. At least," he amended, throwing a quick glance at her nearly second-best gown, "you know more than I do. I need to gather data on the subject, and I cannot just walk around to ask random ladies how important it is to have certain types of fabrics."

"Ah, of course not," Annabelle replied, trying to keep the humor out of her voice. Because she did not want that glower again, but honestly, the thought of him out on the London streets, perhaps carrying a notebook of some sort, and accosting women as they emerged from dressmakers to ask his very detailed, very somber questions, was enough to make her at least want to smirk.

She did not. She was very proud of her self-restraint.

"I will be very pleased to assist you, my lord." A pause, and then she couldn't resist saying, "Even though that task runs far outside the normal duties of a housekeeper, even one who isn't really."

They arrived at his rented house before he could do much more than let out a sharp huff of breath. She'd been hoping for another eye roll, at least, maybe even a tongue sticking out.

A Belle's Guide to Household Management

Cleaning out the house is not the same as being cleaned out, even though by the end of the former your enthusiasm for the task might be the latter.

Chapter Eight

"Oh, and this one! This one is gorgeous; I can just see a young woman, maybe with dark hair, wearing this at her first ball." Miss Tyne leaned back in her chair, the swatch of fabric in her hand, her expression distant. "And he would ask her to dance, and she'd say she wasn't very good at it."

Like making toast, Matthew thought.

"And he'd say, 'All I want is to dance with you in my arms. I don't care if you're good or not.' And he would hold his arms out for her, and she'd step into them, and then they'd dance. All because she was pretty and kind and wore a lovely gown." She shook her head, as though to clear a memory away, then her cheeks flushed a lovely pink color.

They were sitting in the sitting room, the one where Matthew had slept the first night, candles lighting the room up as though it were daylight. He'd only felt a twinge at seeing just how many candles she thought were necessary for them to see by, and he was proud of himself for not snuffing out the ones that were on the desk, rather than at the table at which they were seated. Because he wasn't certain at that point if he wanted to be economical or if he just wanted to be in the dark with her.

"Is this what you were expecting? Me just talking?" she asked, her tone changing to one that held a note of concern. As though he could find her wanting. Maybe he'd find her overabundant in her enthusiasm and joy and beauty and honesty, but not wanting. Never wanting.

Matthew took another swatch from the pile. Unlike Mr. Andrews, he'd parsed them out so he wouldn't overwhelm her eyes. He doubted he could overwhelm her opinion. Thus far, she'd offered comments on no fewer than half a dozen swatches, and there were at least twice that many to go. He'd offered to finish another day, but she'd just shaken her head and kept on going.

"What about this one?" Matthew said, holding the swatch out to her. She took it, but not before touching his fingers with hers, a sly smile on her mouth as though she knew precisely what she was doing.

And she did, didn't she? She'd returned his kiss, she'd told him to hush when he'd tried to offer some sort of honorable excuse. She'd said she wanted it, too, and he couldn't even imagine her lying, especially not about something like that.

He really, really wanted to kiss her again. And perhaps explore other things with his mouth, like the curve where her neck slid into her shoulders or her delicate collarbones or the inside of her wrist.

And more, besides. He wanted to know, rather than just to suspect, what her body might look like, lit by as many candles as she wanted as he just got to look at her. And touch. And be touched by her, her not-a-housekeeper hands trailing all over his skin.

He could imagine she would be just as inquisitive in her lovemaking as she was in her questions about tea and Edinburgh and what he wanted in his life.

And right now, he was perturbed to admit that he knew the answer: her. In fact, he wanted to know all about her, understand how a female came to own any kind of business and what first got her interested in reading and if she'd always spoken so much and been so direct and literal.

He couldn't imagine being able to find any other woman who could possibly fascinate him to such a degree as she had, in such a short amount of time. The thought should have terrified him more than it did, only now he just wanted to discover more of what fascinations she held.

"So what do you think now?" she asked, her eyes still bright with curiosity, even though they had been looking at swatches and discussing what ladies did and did not wish to buy for well over two hours.

Matthew honestly wished ladies would walk around naked, not so much so they'd be on display for him, but because then they wouldn't have this need for fabric, and he could have gone to bed an hour ago.

"I think I don't know what to think," he replied. And wasn't that odd, since it was unusual for him not to know at least how he was leaning in his opinion after so much research.

But it wasn't the fabric or the multitude of papers Mr. Andrews had blessed him with that left him unthinking. Or thinking too hard.

It was her, and damned if he couldn't get her off his mind, as well as other parts of his body. Maybe he'd be happy if she did walk around naked. Although then he would miss the opportunity to watch as she disrobed.

Just now, for example, she was leaning forward, causing the most intriguing gap in her bodice. He could see the shadow between her breasts, the curve of her skin, just enough to make his imagination strip her slowly, each reveal causing more and more of her skin to be exposed to his view.

He needed to think of something else before she realized where his thoughts had turned.

"My lord?" She had reached her hand across the table to clasp his fingers. Perhaps it was too late. Perhaps she knew.

And perhaps that was wonderful.

"Miss Tyne? That is, Annabelle," he said, lifting his hand up to capture her hand, then drawing both their hands back to his chest. He placed her palm flat against his heart, the one that was beating so hard it threatened to pop out of his chest, or at least that was what it felt like.

"Yes, my—" She wrinkled her nose in annoyance. Adorable annoyance, to be sure, but annoyance nonetheless. "I don't know your first name. It seems to me that if someone has kissed someone else, and that someone else is currently holding someone's hand up to a body part, that someone should at least know the other someone's name, and—"

"Matthew," Matthew said, before she could go into any more about names, or their use, or what they meant, or someone kissing someone when all he wanted to do was find out what she would say.

"Matthew." She tilted her head and looked at him, her usual look of curiosity even curiouser, if possible. "Are you named for anyone in particular, or is that just what your parents like? What were your parents like? You mentioned sisters, is your mother alive? Is she in Edinburgh?"

Matthew squeezed her hand. "I was going to ask you a question, Annabelle."

"Of course you were, only I realized I didn't know your name, and then I had to." And then she caught his eye, and her mouth widened into a delicious, intoxicating grin, and she was laughing, her hand still pressed against his chest, the other hand up to her mouth as though to stifle her giggles.

He did not wish to stifle her.

"I'm doing it again, aren't I? Well, fine then," she said, straightening in her chair and donning a very serious expression, belied only by the fact that her eyes were dancing and her mouth kept twitching as she suppressed a smile.

"What do you wish to ask?"

Now that he had her attention, and he honestly wasn't sure how long she could remain silent, he wasn't sure what to say. At this rate, the amount of things that had never happened to him before might overbalance the things he'd come to expect. And he didn't know how he felt about that.

"It seems that there is a...an attraction between us, Miss T—that is, Annabelle."

"Mm-hm," she agreed, as though it was entirely understood and it was entirely normal for them to be discussing it. Was it normal? Did these conversations occur all the time between men and women?

He couldn't worry about that now. Because he had enough to worry about with what was actually happening to be concerned about something he might have missed before.

"And…and it seems as though it would be logical, given our proximity to one another and since I am in London for the next month and that you are, that we did, that…"

"That we kissed?" she supplied helpfully.

"Yes, that, and you can tell, can't you, how your presence is making me feel?"

She pressed her palm harder against his chest, her fingers sliding over the fabric of his waistcoat. Her gaze was locked with his, except for a brief moment when he could have sworn her gaze dipped below the table to…to there.

"I can tell. And I feel the same, Matthew." This time, there was no hint of humor in her voice, for which he was grateful, because if it had seemed as though she were laughing at him, or in any way mocking him, he knew he would have retreated forever, to always be capable, responsible Matthew, not the Matthew who could spontaneously kiss women—or this woman, in particular—against a building in a busy London street.

And he wanted to explore who that other Matthew might be. The spontaneous one, the passionate one, the one who might choose to do something irresponsible, like kiss a woman whom he'd just met, who had, in fact, made his (admittedly burnt) toast that morning.

"So what I would like to know, Miss, Annabelle, is if you'd be interested in continuing to explore our attraction to one another."

A Belle's Guide to Household Management

Also (see "cleaned out"), cleaning up does not, sadly, usually mean you have come into a great fortune. Unless your fortune is measured in dirt, soot, and dust. In which case, you are wealthy beyond measure.

CHAPTER NINE

She couldn't laugh. Even though she really, really wanted to, just for the sheer ridiculousness of it—him sitting over there, all confused and gorgeous and proper, asking her to "explore an attraction," as though it were an exhibit at a museum.

But she knew if she did laugh, even for the right reasons, his lovely mouth would thin out into a hard line and he would close off and be buttoned up for the rest of the month, and she didn't want that to happen, not at all.

What she wanted was for him to stand up, grab her, and pull her to him, putting his mouth to hers in a ferocious, claiming kiss.

But he was far too polite to do that. At least not until she'd told him she wanted it. That. *Him.* And she hadn't told him anything, not yet, even though his question hung in the air like the recently banished dust she'd raised while cleaning the house.

And like the dust, she needed to address it. Only she wouldn't be using her feather duster in this case.

Unless…?

"I would, my lord. Matthew," she amended, smiling as she glimpsed the quick spark of desire that lit his eyes before he glanced away. Was her Scottish earl shy, then?

He hadn't seemed so, but then again, he'd seemed altogether too brusque and remote when she'd first met him. Maybe he was hiding shyness under all that. Maybe he differed from the British aristocracy in his…well, in other things, as well. Because she hadn't noticed him looking at all the women as they'd walked down the street or been in the tavern. He'd just looked at her.

And didn't that give her a delicious feeling!

A feeling she'd never had, not even when she'd thought she was in love, long before she'd fallen. It all had to do with him.

"Yes," she said, to clarify. "I absolutely would."

"Good," he said.

"Matthew," she said as she flattened her palm against his chest, feeling the hard planes of his skin underneath his clothes. *Goodness. What did Scottish earls do to get so fit?* She'd have to ask him. Only not now, not when he was clearly so… so shy about all of this. He might just bolt, and then she'd never get to touch that bare chest for herself.

And she had every intention of doing so, all in the name of exploration, of course.

"Yes, er, Annabelle?" His eyes had darkened, so dark they were nearly black, and suddenly it didn't feel as though she were the one in control. His eyes, the dark passion she saw there, made her mouth dry and a slow, sensual shiver run through her body.

Oh, this was going to be wonderful. Even though it might mean that it ruined her for the rest of her life. Because she could already tell that this man, whether he was Scottish, an earl, a burnt-toast lover, and so much more, was someone she could fall in love with. Even though there would only be that afterward, no promise of anything more. Not that she needed anything more.

She just needed him. Right now.

"Shall we go upstairs?" Her voice sounded lower, softer, and she could have sworn he shook as she spoke.

"Yes, we should." He rose, her hand dropping to the table, but before she could stand as well he had picked her up out of the chair and held her, high against his chest, his wonderful, hard, gorgeous chest, those dark eyes seeming to burn right through her.

She squeaked in surprise as he strode to the staircase, his steps as sure and strong as though she weighed as little as a piece of paper. Or a speck of dust.

"Wait one moment." Annabelle—he should think of her as Annabelle now—waved her hand toward her room, the room where he'd first encountered her, all warm soft female of her. "I need something. Put me down, please."

Matthew lowered her down, his hands sliding down her back, longing to caress her just a bit more, now that he knew that she wanted this, too. That this, whatever *this* was, was going to happen.

Only not, apparently, until she got something from her bedroom. She gave him one last, mischievous glance, and his cock hardened in response. *What was she doing?*

She emerged just a few moments later, an item—*a feather duster?*—in her hand, an even slyer smile on her face.

He swallowed as his gaze traveled between her face and the feather duster and back again. Interesting. He had no idea what she was planning, only that he was guessing—as his cock was as well, it seemed—that whatever it was would be pleasurable. Because it was her, and they were upstairs together alone, and they were about to "explore their attraction." Damned if he didn't sound like his usual stuffy self, only she seemed to like him, and that was a surprise. A welcome surprise.

"Shall we?" she said, waving the duster in the air as she headed to his room. He followed, this throat thick with lust, his hands frantic with the need to touch her.

She stood aside to let him enter, then gave him a quick, appraising look. "Do you even know how handsome you are?" she said, her voice low as though she weren't even talking to him, even though of course she was.

But there was no answer to that, and thank goodness it seemed she didn't expect one.

She tossed the duster onto his bed—*dear lord, his bed*—and stepped forward to him, lifting her arms to wrap around his neck.

"I want you to kiss me some more," she said, her gaze on his mouth.

"Of course," he replied, lowering his mouth to hers. Her lips were soft and warm, and her tongue swept into his mouth and explored, tangling with his as she made a soft noise low and deep in her throat.

His hands were at her waist, and he spread his fingers so they touched the curve of her spine, where her arse met her back. And then traveled lower, squeezing her flesh, kneading it as he pressed his erection against her body.

It felt too good, too soon.

Matthew had explored an attraction before, of course; he wasn't entirely inexperienced, but he'd never before felt this immediate surge of desire, of attraction, of lust, of needing to possess. If he had, he wouldn't still have been a virgin.

The thought of which nearly made him stop. Nearly. Would she laugh when she found out? How would she find out? Was he willing to give that to her, something he'd mentally promised to give first to his future wife?

Only how could he not share something so special with her, the most special woman he'd ever met?

He lost all ability to think, however, when she pulled her mouth from his and pushed him backward, toward the bed.

He shuffled until the back of his knees hit the mattress, then she gave him a harder shove and he fell back, bouncing a few times on the bed.

She tumbled onto the bed on top of him, her eyes sparkling, her mouth red and moist from their kiss.

"Your bed is much nicer than mine." One corner of her mouth tilted up. "Not just because you are in it." She unwrapped his cravat from his neck, then put her hands to his waistcoat and began to undo the buttons, quickly but competently. Then she pushed the two sides of the waistcoat away and began to undo the buttons of his shirt, her face frowning in concentration.

It felt so…unusual, as usual, for her to be here, taking control where normally he was in control. Where he knew every single possible outcome, and had planned accordingly for each one.

He had no idea what would happen next. Right now. As in, he had no idea that after she'd finished with the buttons of his shirt she'd lower her mouth to his neck and kiss it, then lick her way to the lowest part of his chest that was exposed.

He definitely couldn't have predicted just how amazing it felt, to have her body on his, her soft weight pressing him down into the mattress, her mouth on his bare skin.

And how she raised her head and met his eyes, her own gaze focused with a particular kind of desire, of purpose.

He resisted the temptation to close his eyes since he didn't want to miss one possible sense of what was happening. And then realized, of course, he should be exploring, as he'd been given permission to, with his hands, his sense of touch not just restricted to experiencing what she was doing to him.

He placed his hands on her ribcage, the part he could reach that wasn't pressing on him, then spread his fingers out so his thumb and index finger touched the curve of her breast. And then he moved his fingers and she smiled at him, arching into his touch, and it felt amazing, better than any previous explorations had, even though they were both still entirely clothed (although he was now unbuttoned).

"I want to see you with your shirt off. Again," she said with a smirk, and he remembered how it had felt to know she had seen his naked chest, how shocked he'd been at the time.

Only now he wasn't shocked. He wanted her to see him, wanted to see that look of desire in her eye as she regarded him. More, he wanted her to touch him, to run those beginning-to-callous hands over his skin and touch him everywhere. Make him know what it was like to lose control of everything, for every plan and contingency to be forgotten as he gave himself to her.

"You're going to have to move then," Matthew said, nudging her aside with his body. She landed on the bed with a gentle thud. He sat up and flung the waistcoat onto the floor, pulled the shirt over his head, and threw that, as well.

If his housekeeper complained about how messy he was, he could always threaten to put his shirt back on.

"Oh my," she said with a breathy sigh, looking at him so intently it felt almost like a caress on his skin. No, wait, she *was* caressing his skin—she'd reached out to his abdomen and her hand was stroking him, sliding over him as though he were something to be touched, to be handled, not something to be deferred to.

And of course he had to touch her, only she was still wearing clothing. Which did not suit his plans, and he did pride himself on being a planner. Until she had completely upset his carefully plotted course.

But he couldn't think about that now. Not just shouldn't, but couldn't, because all he could think about was her. Specifically, her naked. "Take that off," he said, gesturing to her gown.

"I'll need help," she replied, gesturing to the back. "With the buttons."

She wriggled around and presented her back, looking over her shoulder at him, her expression one of joy and desire and surprise.

He undid the buttons with shaky fingers, then slid the fabric off her shoulders and leaned forward to kiss the nape of her neck. She shuddered as his lips found her skin, and then he pressed more firmly with his mouth, his hands wrapping around her front to slide the gown down until it was at her waist.

She wore more, of course; he hadn't thought it would be so easy to get her naked. He had hoped, certainly, but he'd known that most ladies wore a multitude of clothing. To draw out the suspense of undressing? Or just because they were ladies and liked clothing and fabrics?

This, he reminded himself as he ran his hand over her breasts, still encased in some sort of covering, was research. He had to know what ladies had on under there, didn't he, to know if they would want to purchase silk from exotic lands?

He was well aware he was justifying his actions, but at this moment, he didn't care.

"This, too," he said, tugging on whatever it was she had on under her gown. She stuck her tongue out at him as she leapt off the bed, her gown pooling at her feet, her hands going to laces and fastenings and whatever else there was there until she had taken it all off and stood in front of him, entirely naked.

And smiled, a confident, warm, delicious smile that told him she knew he wanted to look at her, and that he'd like what he saw.

As he did. She curved in at all the right places and curved out at the right places as well. As he watched, she cupped her breast in her hand and flicked her finger on the nipple.

He practically forgot to breathe, it was so erotic. And it was just her touching herself. Imagine what it would be like when it was his hands.

"Come here," he said in a growl, unfastening his trousers and shucking them to the floor to join the rest of their clothing. Now he just had on his smallclothes, and his cock jutted out from the fabric, an obvious sign that their exploration was worth exploring.

She got back onto the bed, bouncing a bit as she sat, a delighted grin on her face. Yes. This was still joyous Annabelle, the one with the thousand questions and the curious mind, the one who, it seemed, was as curious about him as he was about her.

The one who was lushly, gorgeously nude, her pale skin dusted with freckles, like the ones on her nose, her breasts round and full, with rose-colored nipples.

The one who was exploring his chest with her hands, whose eyes were on his mouth, who was pushing him back down and straddling him, those lovely breasts right in front of him. Waiting to be touched.

He did not like to keep anyone waiting.

Matthew raised his hand to her breast, curling his fingers around the soft curve of her, grasping the fullness of her before grazing her nipple with his finger. As she had done.

"Oh," she said with a sigh, then wriggled most interestingly on his body. "I like it when you touch me." A pause as she looked at his body, then wriggled again. "Almost as much as I like to touch you."

And then she slid off him and knelt between his legs, running her hand up and down his cock, like he did when he was alone, only having it be her hand instead of his was much, much better. And, obviously, he was not alone.

She made a low noise in her throat as she stroked him, harder with each pass of her hand. Until she stopped.

"Wha'?" Matthew said, wishing he could complete a word, much less a sentence.

"These should be off," she said, putting her hand to the top of his smallclothes, dragging her nails on his skin. The contact sent shivers through his whole body.

"Yes." Matthew couldn't agree more, and he yanked his smallclothes down and tossed them onto the floor, too.

At this point his housekeeper would be here half the night cleaning his room. Or doing other things.

He preferred the other things.

Now they were both naked, and she smiled and reached out to clasp him in her hand again, and then, and then she leaned forward and licked the top of him and he let out a startled gasp.

"Mm," she said, kissing him more firmly there, then took him into her mouth, the wet warmth of her surrounding him, his mind completely blank of anything but her, her naked body, her joy, her mouth.

A Belle's Guide to Household Management

When a gentleman tells you he is "your servant," that does not mean you are allowed to tell him to go mop the floors.

CHAPTER TEN

She didn't have to wonder anymore just how handsome he was. She knew; he was entirely and thoroughly handsome, from his desire-darkened eyes to his full mouth to his broad chest and then...well, she had to admit, even his manly appendage was handsome.

It tasted musky and throbbed in her mouth, and he was alternately moaning and uttering incoherent noises, so she knew he must have been enjoying it. Because she couldn't see him allowing himself not to speak properly otherwise.

After a few minutes of licking and sucking, she withdrew her mouth but kept her hand on him, drawing her palm up and down the shaft. He was large; to be expected, since he was large everywhere else, too, and he was iron-hard in her hand, but the skin was soft.

She wished she could comment on the discrepancy of soft and hard, but she didn't think this was the time. For once, it appeared, she knew when to keep silent.

And then she wanted to let him know that she, Annabelle, had actually refrained from saying something on her mind because it wouldn't be appropriate. At that time, at least. Perhaps later she could tell him of her observations.

She glanced up at him and he was watching her, watching her move her hand with a sensual look on his face, his chest heaving as his breaths broke loud and gasping in the room.

Good. He was coming undone, and that was just how she wanted him.

She spotted the feather duster on the floor and stifled the grin that threatened to appear on her face. She also knew that grinning at such a point might make him question if she was amused by all of this, and she did not want to lessen the hardness in any way.

Still keeping a hand on him, she slid off the bed, then snatched the duster with one hand and returned to what she was doing, barely missing a stroke.

His eyes were wider now. "What are you planning to do?"

Annabelle did allow herself to grin then, and she ran the duster from the top of his chest down to his cock, flicking the feathers as she went.

He moaned and thrashed, but didn't protest.

"A good housekeeper should always keep everything clean," she said, in as proper a voice she could manage. Given that she had a Scottish earl's cock in her hand, it wasn't very proper at all.

"Of course," he replied, his own tone amused.

She trailed the duster on his strong, muscular thighs, down his legs, and onto his feet. Goodness, even his feet were handsome! Then she drew it back up, making that same feather-flicking motion as her other hand rhythmically stroked his cock.

He groaned, and she glanced at him. Now his eyes were shut, his head was back, and the muscles of his abdomen were standing out as he flexed.

She tossed the feather duster aside and wrapped her other hand around the base of his cock, her fingers sliding over his tight balls as she continued to stroke, now with a firmer grip, now a bit faster.

"Oh, lass, this feels—oh, god," he said, then shouted as he came, his release spurting all over her hand and his torso and his legs.

She smiled and slowly released her hold on him, then moved to lie next to him on the bed, her hand on his chest, which heaved, her face buried into his neck.

"That was…" It sounded as though he was having a hard time speaking. "That was amazing."

"It was an excellent beginning to our explorations," Annabelle replied.

And she couldn't wait to explore some more. Even as she pushed away the thought that she might never wish to stop exploring him. And they had less than a month.

Well. That was amazing. As he'd said already. Wonderful. Tremendous. And many other adjectives Matthew didn't think he had ever thought about anything before.

Another new experience to add to his list of things he'd felt since arriving in London. More specifically, since meeting her.

"I didn't…that is, there is something I could do for you?" He hated how he didn't know, but that was what a virgin was, wasn't it, someone who hadn't done something?

He damned well wanted to find out, though.

She nestled a little closer to him, curling her foot between his legs and caressing his shoulder. He was naked and covered in his own spend, with his housekeeper lying naked next to him.

And he'd never been happier or more comfortable. Wasn't that the most surprising thought of all?

"We can do other things later," she said, a throaty note in her voice. As though she were at that very minute thinking of what he would do to her and relishing the anticipation.

"Good," Matthew said, feeling a warm languor stealing over him. He closed his eyes and just felt, just was, just for the moment. No responsibilities, no one asking him for anything, nothing but her and warmth and the softness of the bed and the softness of her.

When he woke up, he was cold and alone. And it was morning, judging by the light that was streaming through the still-open windows. Matthew sat up, blinking, shaking his head as he tried to remember just—

Oh my. Well, that had happened, hadn't it? And now she wasn't here. He felt an unexpected stab of something in his chest, a tightening that wasn't hunger or anything else he was familiar with. Was she all right? Did she regret what had happened?

He got out of bed and extricated his trousers and shirt from the pile on the floor. He put them on quickly, anxious to make certain she wasn't upset or anything.

It was just to maintain the peace in the household, he assured himself, not because he wanted to see her. Not because he wished to do it all again, and more.

Because, more's the pity, he was still a virgin.

He went downstairs and heard her before he saw her; she was singing something, he couldn't tell what, and she didn't sound upset. He followed the sound and descended the small staircase to the kitchen.

She turned as she heard him enter the kitchen. The sun was behind her, so he couldn't see her face.

"Oh, well, good morning, Miss Ty...that is, Annabelle." And how awkward did he feel now, seeing her, but not certain how she felt? Should he ask her? And how did one ask a lady how she felt the morning after having a shared naked experience with her?

He wanted to attack the problem with his usual logic, but none of this was logical, so he didn't have the first clue.

"Good morning, Matthew," she said, a nuanced something in her voice. She walked up to him and lifted her face up to kiss him.

Well. That answered some questions.

She moved away before he could take her in his arms and kiss her as well, leaving him disappointed and wanting.

"Tea?" she asked, but was already pouring from the teapot into a cup. She set it down on the kitchen table and made a "sit down" gesture. "I'll have the toast ready in a minute."

"Burned in a minute, I think you meant to say," Matthew replied as he sat, feeling that chest-tightening feeling ease. He accompanied his words with a grin, to show he didn't really care about the burnt toast, just in case she thought he was truly upset about it.

Although if she were to be upset about anything, it was what they had done the night before, not the overcooking of bread.

He should say something about it. *Shouldn't he?*

"Uh, and how did you sleep?" *And why weren't you still in my bed when I woke up this morning?*

She smiled and gave him what he thought might be a flirtatious look. "Well enough. Considering someone kept muttering in his sleep."

"Oh." Now he was embarrassed. And when had he ever been embarrassed before? Until now, he would have put the number at zero. Now it was one.

At this rate, his new experience tally might even use all the fingers on an entire hand. With losing his virginity hopefully being one of them.

"Here." She placed the tea in front of him, then frowned as she sniffed the air. "The toast!" she exclaimed, rushing to the oven. She withdrew something from it, and the scent of burning was stronger.

She was consistent in one thing, at least.

"Drat, it's burnt." She glanced over her shoulder at him, an amused expression on her face. "Not only am I not a housekeeper, I am also not a cook."

"I believe we had already established that." Matthew took a sip of his tea. Again, made perfectly for his taste.

That shouldn't have made him feel warm all over—maybe it was just the tea—but it did.

"Are you going to your uncle's office? Are there more of those fabric things for me to look at?"

"Swatches," Matthew corrected. "No, I think I have gotten enough from you."

He winced as soon as the words left his mouth. That wasn't precisely what he meant to say, but it seemed she didn't take offense or misinterpret his meaning.

"Good, because I am going to the market today. I am going to make you something for dinner. And not burnt toast," she added when he opened his mouth to speak.

"We can go out again, if you prefer," he said, relieved it wasn't even a question that they would dine together.

She planted her fists on her hips and regarded him with mock severity. "My lord, if I had wanted to go out again, don't you think I would have said so?" She didn't attempt his accent again, thank goodness.

He smiled, somehow liking it when she teased him. Number three on the list of new experiences.

"I want to make you dinner. Please," she said in a softer voice. She walked to stand next to him and put her fingers in his hair, stroking his head.

It felt wonderful.

"Of course. Thank you. I should be home by five o'clock." He drank the rest of the tea and rose, then slid his arm around her waist and pulled her tight against his body. "Have a good day," he said, lowering his head to kiss her.

She uttered a little noise of surprise, then held onto his shoulders and kissed him back, making him wish he didn't have to go to his uncle's after all, just stay here with her and engage in more explorations.

But if he hadn't come to London on his uncle's business, he would never be here in the first place and never would have met her.

And all too soon he would be leaving, once his business was transacted. Leaving London and her and her mouth and her ability to entrance and confound him all at the same time. Going back to Edinburgh, where his plan was to find a suitable wife, one who was docile and quiet and accepted his logic.

And yet somehow that didn't seem as appealing and as much of a good plan as it had before. Somehow it seemed that he would be losing something when he left here and left her—another new experience for the list.

A Belle's Guide to Household Management

Drawing a bath means bringing water to a bathtub so the master or mistress of the household may bathe. You may, in your own leisure time, draw a bath using pencil and paper, but that will not get anyone in your household clean.

CHAPTER ELEVEN

"So you think it's a good investment?" Uncle Jonas's face was screwed up in concentration as he looked at the preliminary report Matthew had done that morning.

After, of course, seeing his not-housekeeper out of the house to purchase items for their meal tonight.

He really hoped it wasn't toast.

Although honestly, he wouldn't care what it was. Because it would mean they would be spending more time together. Maybe sit together and read, with her only interrupting every minute or so to tell him something.

He imagined that even reading, a usually solitary pursuit, would be companionable with her.

But his uncle was waiting for his answer, not hoping he would muse more about his not-housekeeper. "I do, Uncle." Matthew took a deep breath. "Normally, I base my assessment strictly on the numbers. And these numbers aren't quite as positive as other investments I've recommended. But I've done research"—*research involving a very opinionated, very charming woman who isn't logical in the least*—"and I feel that the intangibles of the investment outweigh the actual numbers as they are on the paper."

"Interesting." His uncle squinted at the paper some more, then waved his hand in dismissal. "Whatever you advise is fine for me. I will have to ask, however, because of the outlay, if you would present your findings to our board. They meet on Valentine's Day. February fourteenth," as though Matthew couldn't figure out the date for himself.

"That is fine, I will prepare something for them."

"And perhaps after that you will dine with us again. We'd grown accustomed to having you here. Miss Delaney was most disappointed that you didn't come to dinner last evening. You did enjoy meeting her, didn't you?"

How was he to answer that? If he said no, he didn't, he would be rude, as well as lying. If he said yes, he had enjoyed meeting her, that would convey a level of interest he simply didn't have.

"I have some things to take care of this evening, Uncle. Thank you for the invitation." There. It wasn't precisely the truth, but it wasn't not precisely. He did have one very important thing to take care of this evening—her.

If he were Annabelle he could explain all of that nuance in perhaps an hour or so. But he wasn't, and he didn't have an hour to spare; he had a meal to return home to and another new experience to, well, experience.

And he had never looked forward to something so much in his entire life.

"Hello?" Annabelle called as she stepped into the agency, noting that the kettle was on. Had she left it going? No, of course not, it had been over a week since she left.

"I'm in here," Caroline called from the office. "How is your Scottish earl?" A pause, then she spoke again. "That is, from your note it sounded as though it was a Scottish earl who had hired you, but I wasn't altogether certain it wasn't a sootyish pearl. But that made much less sense," she finished with a laugh.

Annabelle walked into the office and removed her hat, then flung herself into the chair opposite her friend. "He is…" She paused, then tilted her head.

Caroline's eyes widened and she leaned forward. "Don't tell me. I mean, do tell me."

"What do you mean?"

Caroline made a hmphing sound, then poked Annabelle on the knee. "I have never known you to be at a loss for words. So if you can't think of what to say, then what you have to say must be quite intriguing. What is he like?"

"He's very sensible," Annabelle replied in a repressed tone. "And he is quite smart and interested in what I have to say, and he likes to read Mr. Dickens, and he is quite…pleasant to look at, and he is, oh, well, he is…the thing is…" she continued, hitching her chair a little closer to Caroline, "is that I need one of those things that Lily bought for the ladies."

Caroline's eyes widened more. "A condom? My goodness, how long have you known him?"

I know him. I know he is secretly humorous and altogether handsome and definitely Scottish and obviously stubborn and logical—and I think I am falling in love with him.

I am in love with him.

Only she didn't say any of that. "More than a week," she said defensively.

"More than a week," Caroline repeated dryly. "Are you certain about this? I am glad you are ensuring there will be no accident, if you do plan on doing this, but after a week—"

Caroline's face had a concerned expression, so Annabelle didn't remind her it was more than a week. Just barely, but still. Annabelle knew her friend loved her and didn't want her to fall again. They'd had enough trouble righting her after Charles broke her heart.

"I am certain. I think," and now she could say it out loud, since she'd thought it at least five seconds ago, and that was a lifetime in Annabelle's usual brain-to-mouth speed. "I think I love him."

Caroline peered intently at her, then her face cleared as she saw something, apparently, that satisfied her. Sometimes it was a good thing that everything Annabelle thought went directly to her face. "I think you do, too."

She got up and went to the cupboard and pulled out a paper sack.

"Here you go," she said, handing it to Annabelle. "I hope it is everything you have hoped for."

Annabelle thought of how he'd looked at her the night before and how he'd groaned as he spent and how his mouth kissed her—as though she was the only woman in the world he'd ever kissed or ever wanted to kiss—and how she wanted him to claim her, to bring her pleasure in his bed.

"It will be," she replied, a wicked grin on her face.

A few hours later, she wasn't quite as confident. Because she didn't think he would want to do anything with her if he were hungry—for food, not for her—and right now, regarding the pork chops she'd bought, it didn't seem as though she would be able to feed him properly. Not without resorting to burnt toast.

She heard the door open and her panic increased; he was home, she'd promised him food, and right now she had two quite uncooked pork chops, along with some vegetables, also uncooked, and some wine.

She didn't know if wine was cooked or not, but somehow she doubted it was.

So. An entirely uncooked meal when she'd promised cooking.

"Annabelle?" he said, his voice holding a tone of eagerness she hadn't heard from him before. That made her stomach jump in a lovely way, not in the "I have no dinner for the man I'm planning to seduce" way.

But again, he wouldn't be so eager if he weren't fed.

"I'm in the kitchen," she said, approaching the stove with a purposeful stride. She could do this. She could.

"How is dinner going?" Matthew said as he entered the kitchen. "Are we having toast with oatmeal? Or oatmeal with toast?"

She spun on her heel and looked at him. Goodness, he was so handsome. And he would be hers for a few more days. If he didn't starve to death in the meantime.

"Pork chops. I think," she added, just in case he was going to get his hopes up too high.

"You think?" he asked, approaching the stove. "Do you need me to light this?"

She crossed her arms over her chest and made a harrumphing noise.

"You know how to? Are all Scottish earls so competent, or is that something you've taken on as some sort of personal challenge?"

He laughed, and that sound, so rare in their acquaintance, made her heart beat a little faster and made her want to hear it some more.

Hopefully, however, he wouldn't laugh when he ate dinner, because then it would likely be in a bad way, and she was hoping to feed him enough so he'd have energy for later on.

For later on when she loved him. Literally, as well as figuratively.

"I just know how to," he said with a shrug. He took the matches from beside the stove and lit it, just as he'd said he could.

"And the pan? Did you find one?" He glanced at the wall, where a few pans hung from hooks.

"A pan! Of course!" Annabelle scrambled onto the counter, then lifted one of the pans off the wall and hopped down, holding it out to him.

"So, if I'm not mistaken, we put the chops into the pan, put them over the heat, and cooking occurs." His voice was amused, and she was relieved he wasn't irritated at her inability to cook.

Then again, she'd told him she wasn't a cook, so he couldn't have been expecting much. She knew it was likely to be a disaster, but she'd wanted to do something for him, something that was here in the house they were sharing—albeit for only a short period of time—something that was lovely and companionable and very domestic.

While the chops sputtered in the pan, he chopped the vegetables and directed her as to how to open the wine bottle and set the table. And every so often they'd bump into one another and she'd glance at him, and something in his gaze would make her breath catch and think about later, after dinner, and what she had gotten from Caroline.

"Dinner's ready," he said after about fifteen minutes of pan-sputtering and glance-sharing and wine-opening.

The chops were good and the wine was better, and soon Annabelle didn't feel foolish about any of it, especially when he looked so satisfied, but also hungry, and this time for her.

"Stop looking at me like that," she said in a low voice.

"Like what?" he took a sip of wine and then licked his lips, and Annabelle knew the exact same look of desire was on her face.

"Like I am dessert."

He raised one eyebrow. "I hadn't thought of that, but now that you mention it, perhaps we could move straight to dessert?" And he stood and held his hand out to her, and she rose and took it, then let him guide her up the stairs, through the hallway, up the stairs again, and down the hallway to his room.

To his bed.

A Belle's Guide to Household Management

Mopping the floor with someone is quite different from just mopping the floor.

CHAPTER TWELVE

Now that it was finally about to happen, Matthew felt nervous. Nervous he wouldn't please her, nervous it wouldn't live up to his expectations.

Nervous that he'd never want to do this with anyone but her, ever again.

"It feels odd, having come up here just for this purpose," she said as she faced him, beginning to untie his cravat. Her eyes were focused on what she was doing. Until she paused and looked up at him, her expression so direct it made him shiver.

"That is, I suppose I should be coy and pretend I don't want this, but I don't pretend—I can't; and we only have a little more time before you return to Scotland, and I want to do this as often as we can, and I already miss you." She looked back down and finished the cravat removal, tossing it onto the floor.

He swallowed against the lump in his throat. "I suppose I miss you already, too," he said stiffly, wishing he could be as guileless as she was. Not that he lied, but he had difficulty expressing emotions.

Likely because usually he didn't have any, beyond annoyance that he had to explain something that seemed perfectly clear.

But with her, he had many more emotions: he felt joy and happiness and warmth and desire and satisfaction.

He felt what it was like to be human.

Is this what it all felt like? That thing he'd never expected to have?

It seemed she understood what he meant, because she didn't pull away or react as though he hadn't just opened his heart to her. Because he had, oh he had, as much as he was able to.

That was item number six, wasn't it?

"Then I suppose we should agree that this is what we are here to do, and you should kiss me. Now," she added, as though either one of them would delay it.

He had never followed orders before—item number seven; at this rate he might have to move on to count numbers on his toes—but he did now, lowering his head to hers as he slid his hands around her waist, pulling her to him so their bodies pressed together.

His cock was already erect, and when it made contact with her stomach she made a soft moan in her throat that told him she liked what she felt.

And he did as well. Except there were far too many layers of clothing between them.

His fingers moved to the back of her gown and began to undo the buttons, still kissing her deeply, sliding his tongue inside her mouth, sucking on her tongue, coaxing more of those low growls from her throat.

Meanwhile, he'd gotten enough of the buttons done so he could slide his hand onto her back, now covered in one less layer of fabric. He slid his fingers lower, onto her arse, and squeezed, which pressed more of him into her.

She broke the kiss, gasping, a look of impatience on her face. "We need to remove our clothing because I will expire if I cannot feel you, all of you, on all of me."

He very much appreciated how direct and honest she was at this moment.

Both of them began to undo buttons and slide fabric off shoulders and hips, and flung clothing onto the floor as though nothing else mattered but the speed of the task.

Which, judging by how he felt, and how he presumed she felt, was the truth.

She took longer than he did, of course, so he got onto the bed and watched her.

She glanced at him from under her lashes, a knowing, sensual smile on her mouth. "Touch yourself," she said, her motions slowing as she slid her undergarment off her shoulder, revealing one breast.

"Touch my—"

She licked her lips. "Yes, touch your cock. Stroke it how you want me to stroke it."

His breath caught at hearing her say the word, a word he'd never heard anyone say before, much less a woman. A lady, even, despite her not having a title. She was elegant and kind and funny and lovely and generous and honest. That was a lady.

Matthew reached around himself and began to stroke up and down his shaft, still watching her. And she was watching him, still undressing, but slower, as though putting on a show.

She was bared to the waist now, and as he kept sliding his hand up and down himself, she pushed the fabric down her legs and onto the floor, leaving her entirely naked.

And not on the bed with him.

"Get up here." He barely recognized his voice, it was so low and raspy.

She crawled onto the bed on her hands and knees, her gorgeous, full breasts swaying, her gaze locked on his face.

"Now what do you want?" she asked in a whisper. "Do you want me to touch you? Do you want me to lick you? Or maybe I could find my feather duster and show you how very much not a housekeeper I am?"

"Yes," he said in a groan, reaching for her, claiming her mouth in a ruthless, savage kiss.

She held onto his shoulders and pushed him back onto the bed so she lay on top of him, his cock nestled between her thighs, her breasts pressing into his chest.

It was too much, and yet it wasn't enough.

He ran his hands down her back and onto the soft curves of her arse, then back up again, loving how she was touching him as well, her hands caressing his neck, his shoulders, sliding down his arms and then grasping his arse, squeezing it. She was moving her body slightly atop his, her breasts rubbing against his chest, her mound against his erection.

He wanted to devour her, he wanted to know what it felt like to be inside her, to bring her to climax as she'd done him the previous night.

Suddenly she sat up, still straddling him, a frown on her face.

No. What? Had he done something wrong?

"I need to get something," she said, hopping off the bed. She gestured to him. "You can keep all that going, I'll be right back."

It didn't seem as though he'd done anything wrong, judging by her face. And she had given him a direction he was more than pleased to comply with, so he grasped himself in his right hand and began to stroke the shaft, closing his eyes, imagining it was her hand on him.

Within about a minute she'd returned, holding something, which she held out to him. "This is for you. So that when we...when..." she said, her eyes alight with desire and want and perhaps something else?

"Ah." He knew what it was, of course. He just hadn't used one before, and wasn't entirely sure what to do. It appeared simple enough, however, so he took it and began to roll it down over his cock.

"Let me help," she said, getting back onto the bed and guiding the material down over him until it was at the very bottom.

Then she lay down next to him on her side and her hand began to stroke and play with the hair on his chest, her palms pressed flat against the muscles, her leg flung over his.

And then she reached lower and tugged on him. "I want you inside me," she said in a soft voice so low it was hard to hear.

"We agree then," he said in return, liking how she chuckled, even as she grabbed his arse and pulled, to indicate he should lay on top of her.

He got onto his knees and gazed down at her, at her body, her face, which had an intense expression as she met his eyes.

"Now, Matthew," she said, taking his penis in her hand and guiding him toward her body.

He entered her, just a bit, and it felt so incredible already he had a brief moment of worry he would spend right there. Or die of excitement before getting completely inside.

But she hooked her legs around him and pushed him in farther and farther, until he was buried inside her, his face against her neck, her breathing rough and ragged against his ear.

"You can move, if you want," she said, an amused tone in her voice.

He wasn't certain he could.

She shifted her hips and pulled him against her, then let go so he was released just a bit, at which point he realized that if he didn't move, he would die.

And he did not wish to die, not right now, not until he'd finished.

So he raised himself up on his arms and hovered above her, his eyes focused on her face, moving slowly, the sound of their breathing the only sound in the room.

"Faster," she said, grabbing his hips and guiding him in and out.

It had felt incredible before, but now it felt even more incredible. Matthew didn't think there was even a word for how good it felt to have his cock sliding in and out of her, her hands on his body, her breasts jiggling as their bodies moved together.

It went on for a lifetime, or at least five minutes, and then he felt a gathering pressure, an intensity, and he then he exploded, the orgasm overwhelming his entire body as he pushed, hard, into her, collapsing on top of her as the ripples of pleasure rushed through him.

When he could speak, perhaps a lifetime (or five minutes) later, he lifted his head and met her gaze. "That was incredible."

She returned his smile. "It was, wasn't it?"

"But you didn't—" he began, not quite sure how to broach the subject.

She shook her head. "No, but I did enjoy myself. It is much rarer for ladies to achieve all that during, hasn't that been your experience?"

"This is my first time," he replied.

Her eyes widened and she tried to sit up, only he was still lying on top of her, so instead she merely squirmed.

"Your first? That is, me?" Her words came out in a startled squeak.

"Mm-hm."

"But you're a man!" she exclaimed.

He laughed and said, "It's good you noticed that, otherwise I would have to think I was terrible. Being a man doesn't guarantee anything."

"And an earl!" she added, still not seeming to comprehend what he'd told her.

"A Scottish earl, don't forget," he said with a chuckle. "And now that we've established who I am, let us move on to you." He slid out of her and returned to his knees, taking the condom off and leaning down to grab his cravat from the floor. He wrapped it up in the fabric and dropped it to the ground.

"You are lovely," he spoke in a low voice, putting his fingers on her shins and sliding them up her legs. He bent his head down and kissed first one foot, then the other. Then moved to her ankles. "And absolutely intriguing," he continued, moving up to her knees, kissing both in turn, "and curious," at which point he ran his hands up to her breasts and grasped them, rubbing his fingers over her erect nipples, "and delicious," he said, before lowering his mouth to her sex and licking and kissing her there as he had her mouth.

She let out a gasp and buried her fingers in his hair, holding him to her, her soft cries letting him know what she liked. He licked her, burrowed his tongue inside her, reveled in the taste of her, how her moans were coming faster and faster, nearly in time with his licking.

He drew the little button at the apex of her sex into his mouth and sucked on it, causing her to cry out, then released it to lick her thoroughly, keeping the rhythm consistent as she had with her hand on his cock.

It seemed that was working, because she began to utter one long, continuous moan until she spasmed and screamed his name, her legs twisting all around him, his mouth on her until her body subsided.

"Oh my goodness," she said at last in one breathy sigh. "That was incredible."

He grinned, feeling quite proud of himself, then raised up and returned to lie next to her, gathering her in his arms and kissing her forehead, her head, touching her body with light, idle strokes.

"If you…if this was your first time, then how did you know?" her hand twirled in the air to fill in her missing words.

"Study. You wouldn't cook a recipe without consulting a book, would you?" He paused. "Then again, you would."

She swatted him on the arm. "That must have been some studying you did."

"I'm very glad you enjoyed the results of my long and arduous dedication to the subject," he said, kissing her mouth again.

"Mm-hm," she replied. "But you have to let me up."

"Fine, I will," he said, moving off her, but tucking her in close to his body, "but this time don't leave me," he said before he fell asleep.

A Belle's Guide to Household Management

Despite what you might have heard, a whistle is not particularly clean. Do not use it to gauge the state of your home.

She didn't leave. Even though she was absolutely startled and wanted to wake him up to ask him questions about why not and why her and why now, but she knew that he wouldn't be able to answer her satisfactorily, plus it didn't really matter, except it did, because it was him and her, and she hadn't even thought it was a possibility.

Plus there was how he'd brought her pleasure, even though it was his first time, and she wondered just how good he'd be at it in ten more tries, or fifty, and then got melancholy that the fiftieth time wasn't likely to be with her.

She didn't think she'd ever do it again now that she had done it with him. Not that he'd ruined her for anybody else, precisely; it was just that being with him had shown her how good it could be when you loved someone. And it wouldn't be fair or honest to do all this with anybody else.

But what was she doing, anyway? She was lying in bed with her employer, a man who was going to be leaving soon, and taking her heart with him.

And even though she had so many other questions, on this fact she was absolutely certain: that she loved him, and now he'd ruined her for anyone else.

Damn it.

But this was all part of life, wasn't it? And she couldn't get all mopey and ruin the short amount of time they had together.

And the day after tomorrow was Valentine's Day, and even if he had no clue about the holiday or, what was more likely, thought it was a foolish holiday, she had a Valentine for once, one who made her feel special and desired, even if just for a little while.

"Wake up, Annabelle." The words were accompanied by some sort of soft touch on her breasts. She opened her eyes to see him holding her feather duster, the feathers lightly stroking her nipples. It felt absolutely luxurious, but also funny because it was him—a very naked him—holding something so odd for him to hold, a look of intense concentration on his face.

"Good morning," she said, reaching up to caress his cheek. "I'm still here, as you asked."

His eyes traveled down her body, then back up to meet her gaze. "I see that. And I am very pleased." He trailed the duster down over her belly, then onto her thighs.

It tickled, but not in an agonizing way; more of a prolonging-the-delightful-pleasure way. He continued working the duster over her body, trailing the feathers across her lightly, his cock stiffening against her hip.

"Maybe you are the real housekeeper here," she said with a grin, then pulled him onto her and kissed him until he dropped the duster and used his fingers and his mouth on her instead.

"Don't you have meetings today?" It was about an hour later, and Annabelle was completely and totally sated; he'd seen to that. It seemed he was making up for lost time.

"No, I have a meeting tomorrow." He frowned, as though thinking, then looked at her. "I am wondering—would you be able to attend the meeting with me? I have to speak with the potential investors of the silk company, and I'm not certain... actually, never mind, I know... I cannot speak with the same enthusiasm and authority you can."

"Really? You want me to attend a business meeting?" Somehow that trust made it feel as though her heart were going to burst through her chest. He knew she wasn't a housekeeper, he definitely knew she wasn't a cook, and yet he wanted her to come speak to a group of business men about something she did know about.

She loved him even more then.

"Yes, if I didn't want you to attend, I wouldn't have asked you." He spoke in his usual entirely practical way. "Naturally." He paused, and when he spoke again, it was much more hesitantly. "So, will you come with me?"

"Of course," she said. "Only what are we going to do today?" Because tomorrow was tomorrow, and it sounded as though she had one entire day to spend with him, and she knew once his business was concluded he would likely return to Edinburgh and she would never see him.

And she couldn't think about that right now or she'd cry and ruin their day together.

Of course he could have spent the day much more practically: going over his presentation, or working on his other business affairs, things that didn't require he be in London, or even write some delayed letters to his sisters and his mother. But he didn't want to. Another first.

He wanted to spend the day with Annabelle, hear her laugh, feel her almost palpable joy, perhaps steal a kiss when they were out walking.

So they decided to walk to the National Gallery and look at art, something he would have rolled his eyes at if someone had told him he would do and actually enjoy. On the way there they stopped at a bookstore and spent an hour browsing, discovering they both liked stories with lots of dialogue, nothing too sad, and filled with colorful characters. He bought her a few books, wishing he would be able to sit in a room with her somewhere and read with her, only knowing they couldn't.

The National Gallery was relatively empty, and they could stroll together, arm in arm, Matthew feeling a contentment he didn't think he'd ever had.

She paused in front of a painting and pointed to it with one hand while squeezing his arm with the other. "This one is lovely, don't you think? The way the colors of the sky all sort of blend together, and how the cows look so peaceful."

His enjoyment of the art was due in no small part to her enthusiasm over the works. And she was enthusiastic, spending a good half hour looking at a picture that appeared, to Matthew's view, to be a few hills and a farmhouse.

But when she spoke about it, he could see its beauty, could almost feel the waving grass and see the puffy clouds, with all the tiny people working in the fields, and achieve a bit, he thought, of her emotions seeing the painting.

How wonderful must it be to see everything through that joyful lens? Although he was starting to, wasn't he, beginning with seeing her as the epitome of joy? And now that he'd seen her like this, he didn't want to stop looking.

What was he going to do about that?

His practical mind was screaming at him to stop speculating about the future, that nothing could continue between them. But his practical mind, heretofore the only mind he'd thought he had, was being drowned out by his newly discovered romantic mind.

He didn't want to let her go. Ever. He wanted her and her joy in his life, not to mention his bed, forever.

"And these flowers! My goodness, they are lovely." They had walked to stand in front of a painting depicting a vase of flowers. Apparently lovely flowers, according to her.

Matthew glanced around but saw no one nearby, so he slid his arm around her waist and pulled her to him, lowering his mouth to kiss her. Not a long, passionate kiss, that would be foolish, but just something to try to express how he was feeling without saying anything.

Given that he was accustomed to saying precisely what was on his mind, it was hard not to just tell her, but—for the first time, number eight—he was unsure of what exactly he wanted to say beyond "I love…"

The realization hit him like he'd been struck by lightning. Of course. Of course he loved her. That explained all the unexplainable emotions and feelings he'd been having since he met her. That explained why he didn't want to leave her, ever, and why just spending the day with her felt like the most fun he'd had in his life.

And the nights…well, those were pleasurable as well.

"Matthew, are you all right?" she said, gazing up at him as he still held her against his body.

No, I'm not. I'm in love with you.

"I am fine. Tell me, what are your favorite flowers?" he said, turning them back so they were once again looking at the painting.

"Definitely roses. Or no, maybe daffodils. Or peonies. I do like irises, even though they seem so gawky, standing so straight and tall." She laughed, and met his gaze. "It is so typically me, isn't it, that I just love all flowers."

"It is," he replied, tightening his grip on her waist.

And I love you for it.

A Belle's Guide to Household Management

The housekeeper is the mistress of her domain, but she is not the mistress of her master, even though he pays her for her services, is able to tell her what, when, and how to do them, and requires her to dress appropriately.

Chapter Fourteen

"I will not be making dinner tonight." Annabelle clutched Matthew's arm as they strode home. They'd gotten tea at a restaurant near the museum, and Annabelle felt so proud to be in the company of such a good-looking man. She'd caught a few of the ladies nearby looking at him, and she wanted to get up and stick her tongue out at each of them, taunting them with the knowledge that she was the only woman ever to lie with him.

But that would be entirely inappropriate. So she just smiled knowingly as the ladies accidentally caught her eye, and that seemed to convey just about the same thing.

"I don't want you to make dinner either," he said in a sly tone. "Mostly because I don't want you to cook. Nor do I want to cook."

She swatted him on the arm and laughed. "Fine, I am a terrible cook. Shall we eat at the same place as before, or do you want to wander to find someplace new?"

He looked down at her and smiled, a smile that made her heart do a few flips inside her chest. "I'd like to wander."

She grinned and made a sweeping gesture with her other hand. "We will wander, then."

They walked together in silence, but it was a lovely, companionable silence. Annabelle kept wanting to say something about how she felt, but she didn't want to make him uncomfortable, not on their day together. So while she opened her mouth frequently, she didn't speak, because how would she say anything without saying it entirely? "I've fallen in love with you over the course of a week, and I want to be with you and your strong, handsome chest and your very sly wit for the rest of my life." *What could he possibly say to that?*

Even though not saying something usually ended up in her saying something worse. She'd have to try to prevent—

"Oh, look!" She stopped in front of a shop window, one with an array of Valentine's Day cards, each more fulsome and ridiculously gaudy than the rest.

Of course she loved all of them.

"They have a lot of cards in the window." Matthew spoke as though he were reporting on facts, not marveling at the beauty and splendor of them. Of course.

"Yes, Valentine's Day is tomorrow."

She felt him shrug.

"It's a holiday for people who don't know what to say the rest of the year. Why can't they just say how they're feeling? It would save a lot of money."

Practical Matthew. If she weren't well aware of who he was and how he felt about impractical things, she would feel suddenly sad that he cared for the day so little.

As it was, her heart only fell a little bit.

"That's right, you would likely say, 'I care about you very much, how can you not possibly comprehend that? If I did not care for you, I would say so.'" She lowered her voice to mimic his.

"Yes. That is what I would say," he replied, without a hint of humor.

Had she offended him? On their day together? Now her heart really was sinking.

"I only meant—"

"Let's go find a place to eat. I find I am suddenly quite hungry." He began to walk quickly away from the shop, dragging her with him.

She wished she could tell him how that made her feel, too. But she couldn't tell him that without admitting the other.

Thank goodness they would be eating soon, so she couldn't speak. Now if they could just continue that for the remainder of their time together, she would escape with her heart only a little trampled.

Valentine's Day. Tomorrow had to be Valentine's Day, didn't it? And he hadn't remembered, since why would he, the day had never meant anything to him before. But he hadn't missed how her face lit up when she saw all the cards, and he knew that the day was significant, especially to lovers.

And they were lovers now.

Of course it would be the day he'd asked her to attend a business meeting, of all things, with every intention of leaving London soon thereafter.

On the other hand, if he were to do something he'd never done (number nine!), and indulge in an extravagant, romantic gesture, perhaps she would consider returning to Scotland with him. As his countess.

Even though she was nothing like the woman he'd imagined finding in six months, a solid, dependable woman who was never foolish, spoke little, and could likely make toast. Nothing like the woman he had, quite unexpectedly, fallen in love with.

The woman he'd do any number of foolish things for if it meant he could have her forever.

"I need to see my uncle before the meeting." Matthew had been more brusque that morning, only kissing her for a few minutes before looking at the clock and scowling.

It was as though yesterday and last night had never happened, and they'd returned to being just earl and housekeeper.

Although Annabelle didn't think it was usual for an earl's housekeeper to be admiring her employer's backside as he dressed. So perhaps not quite like that.

Even though she was already mourning his loss, at least right now she could enjoy the view.

"Shall I meet you there, then?" she said, sitting up in bed. "What time is the meeting? And what do I have to do?"

He turned to meet her gaze, his hands wrapping his cravat around his throat.

"You just have to be yourself," he said warmly, and Annabelle felt herself relax at his tone. Perhaps he was just anxious about the meeting, not regretting whatever they'd done so far. "The meeting is at two o'clock; I'll leave in about an hour so I can speak with my uncle."

It sounded as though speaking with his uncle was very important, since he'd mentioned it twice in the space of two minutes. It wasn't like him to repeat himself; he must be anxious. That was it. It wasn't her.

But even as she reassured herself, she was conscious that each minute meant one less minute with him, and that was enough to make her anxious, too.

She arrived at the building proclaiming it to be MacIntyre and Sons at fifteen minutes to two, having given herself plenty of time to get distracted by shop windows along the way.

Only she hadn't been very distracted—she'd seen many more windows showing Valentine's Day wares and had gotten sad and turned away, rather than linger as she usually did.

Which was foolish; it wasn't as though she'd had any expectation of the day. But it hurt to see so many people walking arm in arm, flowers everywhere, smiles and happiness and couples who were going to be together in a week's time, not separated by a country and their class and their futures.

She shook off her feelings of melancholy as she walked into the building; she couldn't fall short of his expectations, no matter how much the day had fallen short of hers.

As it happened, Matthew was still with his uncle at two o'clock, and it was another half an hour before the meeting began, long enough for Annabelle to get nervous. But then

Matthew escorted her into the meeting room and sat her so gently into a chair and made sure she got tea, and then he began the meeting by talking about all sorts of things Annabelle had no clue about—investments, outlay, risk, supply chains, and things that she supposed were business terms. She was a business owner, but she left all the details to Caroline, whose mind was much better suited for it.

At last, it was her turn.

"Miss Tyne is here to offer the feminine perspective." Matthew looked at her, and she could have sworn he winked. She would not have thought Matthew was a winker. "Miss Tyne?"

She rose, holding the swatches of fabric she'd first seen. *Was it only a few days ago?* It felt as though it were a lifetime. The men—there were perhaps half a dozen of them, all older than Matthew, of course none as handsome—regarded her as they had Matthew, and waited for her to speak.

"Fabric might seem as though it is just fabric, gentlemen." She held up one of the swatches. "And perhaps you just see some flowers on a blue background. And that is what is here, on the surface." She stroked one of the flowers on the material. "But this material represents opportunity."

She held the swatch up. "For some lucky woman, having this fabric made up into a gown could be an opportunity to change her life. Perhaps she wears the gown to a dinner party or a ball; perhaps she feels lovely in the gown and therefore she looks the best she ever has. Perhaps some nice gentleman"—*one who is tall and dark-haired and with a lovely, lovely chest*—"sees her and finds her enchanting. He begs for an introduction, they dance, and then they are married. And have at least five children." *All of whom would be practical and yet able to be nonsensical at times as well.*

"Or this one," she said, swapping out the swatch for one in a pale cream. "Perhaps this would be worn by a debutante at her coming out ball, and it is her first time to be an adult and move in the adult world, and she conducts herself impeccably and ends up a duchess. Not married to one of the current dukes, mind you, because they are all old and married already, but perhaps…"—and at this she shot a quick glance at Matthew, who was smiling at her—"a Scottish duke, since we know the Scottish nobility are quite different from ours."

"So you see," she said, putting the swatch down again, "pretty fabric will always be pretty, but it also represents an opportunity for beauty and a fulfilling life. Thank you."

She nodded and sat back down, pleased with herself for not having gotten off the subject too much.

"Thank you, gentlemen." Matthew's uncle beamed. "I look forward to our vote about this opportunity," and at that he winked at Annabelle. Perhaps it was a family trait. "But it seems fairly clear what we should do."

The men rose and filed out of the room, eventually leaving just Matthew and Annabelle.

"You were compelling," he said, running his hands down her arms. "Even I wanted to wear a pretty gown after you spoke, just to see what opportunities might present themselves."

If only this was an opportunity and not something that was coming to an inexorable end.

A Belle's Guide to Household Management

That said, if the master of the house does not currently have a mistress, and he wishes you to apply for the position, just ask him what position he would like you in. And then apply yourself.

CHAPTER FIFTEEN

Matthew held the door of MacIntyre and Sons open for her as she stepped onto the sidewalk. He put her bonnet, which had apparently gotten tilted, to rights, then gazed at her, his eyes dropping to her mouth.

"Let us go home, and you can help me pack. I can't imagine Uncle Jonas needing my assistance for much longer, and I've neglected my business being here." *Being with her.*

"Of course, only—" She bit her lip and wished she could say just what was on her mind: *Don't go, take me with you, I love you.*

"What?" he asked, sounding impatient.

"Just that I would like to take you to…"—she scrambled in her brain for something to say, just something to prolong this time with him, to keep him with her, out here on this perfect day for just a few more minutes—"to St. James's Palace, where the Queen was married." She winced at that, hoping he wouldn't think that she was angling to get married. *I just want to spend more time with you.* "And I don't think you've seen many sights since you've been here; you've been too busy working." *And being with me.*

"You're certain you don't want to go home?" Now he sounded quite impatient, and her heart hurt; was he so desperate to have this end? Because as soon as it was their last night—and she wasn't sure if that was tonight or the next, but it was soon—it would all be over, and she knew she would never, ever be the same.

"No, I really think you should see the palace." She spoke as firmly as she could, and he regarded her for a few heart-stopping moments before nodding his head.

"Fine, the palace." He quickened his pace, and she had to scamper to keep up with him.

In a few moments, though, it seemed he realized what he was doing. "Sorry, Annabelle," he said, a shy smile on his lips, "I'm not accustomed to being with anybody."

"I know," she replied with an arch of her brow.

And now he looked discomfited. She leaned into him and whispered in his ear. "I am so lucky to have been your first."

She saw a slow flush climb onto his cheeks, and she wished she could just kiss him out here, in front of everybody.

"Speaking of that business," he said. "You were not—that is, what—?"

"How was I an unmarried woman and yet not in your situation?" She had been tempted to let him try to fumble through what he was trying to say, but couldn't bear to see him so uncomfortable.

"Yes, that. That is, you are, well you are you, and clearly more than a...a not-housekeeper, and it seems as though you should be married already or something. Although that would mean, of course, that we wouldn't be here."

His face was positively red now. She stifled a laugh, which at least was doing something to assuage the grief she was already feeling at having to leave him.

She tightened her hold on his arm. "You might have noticed that I am a bit…literal when it comes to things. I believe people are good and speak honestly." She shrugged and tried to make herself sound as nonchalant as possible. "A man told me he loved me, that he would marry me, and I trusted him." She paused and took a breath. "It turns out that only one of the things he said was true. He did love me, in his way, I believe. But he never intended to marry me."

She felt the muscles in his arm tighten, and it made her wish that Charles were here so Matthew could take a swing at him, even though that likely made her a very bad person. But she would like to see Matthew flatten him.

"I am sorry for that, Annabelle," he said in a soft, low voice.

She gave a quick shake of her head, trying to blink away the sudden sting of tears. "It's fine. Going through it meant I met my friends, and then we started the agency, and then…" *And then I met you, and it was all worth it. Even though you are leaving.*

"I don't wish to see the palace after all," he said abruptly. "I want us to go home."

She felt her heart squeezing, her chest constricting. She probably had less than two days left with him. Forty-eight hours. How many minutes would that be?

Dear God, she was in a bad way if she was resorting to doing mathematical calculations.

In far too short a time they were on Grove End Road, and Annabelle recalled how it had been not so long ago when she'd arrived, expecting a certain kind of man, an earl, with certain duties, and having none of that happen. And yet all of it happened, and she wanted to pinch herself.

She really never would be the same, would she? Damn it.

He fumbled with the key at the door, her capable earl suddenly seeming to get quite clumsy.

"Here, you unlock it," he said.

She took the key and turned it in the lock, then pushed the door open.

And stepped into a room of flowers. More flowers than she'd seen in her entire life. More flowers than she knew existed in the world.

Daffodils—*where had he gotten those?* Roses, peonies, irises, and all the other ones she hadn't named but were her favorite flowers nonetheless. Because she loved all flowers. And that is what he had gotten for her.

And a table covered with cards. Cards enough for the entire lineage of Tynes, trimmed with ridiculously exuberant decorations, such as lace and ribbons and hearts and cupids, and arrows and enormous, swirling calligraphy proclaiming love in at least three languages. Maybe more, she wasn't sure.

And an enormous basket of fruit, including items she knew full well were out of season.

Plus a stack of books.

She turned to look at him, and he had the most lovely smile on his face.

"What? How did…?"

"Do you like it?" he asked, then shook his head. "Of course you like it, how do I have to even ask, your joy is written all over your face. That is one of the reasons I love you. I never have to guess what you're thinking."

He closed the door, then drew her into his arms and spun her so her back was against his chest.

He loved her? He loved her. He loved her!

Her heart was racing and her breath caught, and she wanted to laugh and cry and demand to know what he'd done and why and kiss him until she couldn't kiss him anymore.

"I have a very important question to ask you, Annabelle." His arms tightened. "Or two, actually."

He released her, then walked to stand in front of her. He was even more gorgeous than all the flowers.

He took her hands and placed the palms against his chest. "Do you feel my heart? Wait, that's not one of the questions," he added, with a baffled look on his face. "See what being around you does to me? Not one of the questions, either."

He took a deep breath. "Annabelle, will you be my Valentine? That is one of the questions."

She smiled and nodded. "I will, thank you. I want to be your Valentine more than anything else in the world."

"Good, good," he said, as though distracted. As though he were her, although right now she could not think of anything but him. "Just a moment, let me get something." He removed her hands from him, then turned abruptly and opened the door to the closet. He bent down and turned back around, now with a grumpy Cat in his arms.

"Oh, Cat!" He rolled his eyes as she spoke her cat's name. Well, what did he think she was going to name her? Feline?

Her heart swelled, even as she wondered how he'd managed to discover where Cat was and had gotten her here without Annabelle noticing. But he was beyond clever; he could do anything, couldn't he?

It was as though he'd read her mind.

"You want to be my Valentine more than anything else in the world?" he said as he dropped to one knee, letting Cat go, who immediately went and twined about Annabelle's legs. He drew a box from his pocket and withdrew the gaudiest ring Annabelle had ever seen in her entire life. "Now that I have your answer to that, I want to ask you something else. Annabelle, will you marry me?"

And for once in her life, Annabelle was speechless.

Until she was finally able to stop kissing him and say, "Yes."

EPILOGUE

Of course they didn't precisely have a plan, because it was Annabelle, and the most she seemed to plan was the next time she could get him naked and on top of him—or him on top of her, she didn't seem to have a preference—but beyond that, she just was happy and joyous and he loved her.

He loved her so much; he loved how her face brightened when she saw him, even if he wasn't naked at the time, and how she poked fun at how orderly he was and told him how handsome he was, so much he felt himself blushing.

But they had decided they would spend half of their time in Scotland, tending to his estate, while she dealt with the agency's affairs via the post, and then they would head to London, where he could consult with his uncle on the new shipping ventures and she could continue to work at the agency, although he forbade her from actually taking any postings herself. He knew how adorable she was, and he didn't want any other men seeing her and trying to take her from him.

Not that she'd be taken, except by him; she said as much, and at certain times she begged him to take her, and at those times he was only too happy to oblige.

This was only a temporary position, she assured him, since she knew it would be seen as odd, very odd, for a countess to continue working, but then he'd pointed out that she would be a Scottish countess, and somehow that made it all right, at least in her eyes.

And, he said with a dark promise in his eyes, she'd soon enough be having little Scottish children with him.

Which required lots and lots of lovemaking.

They were back in London, having returned from Scotland where he'd introduced her to his family. His sisters, naturally enough, adored her, and his mother melted when Annabelle insisted on making her tea just the way she liked.

She had just brought him tea as well, putting it down on the desk he was working on. He hoped he could lure her to bed soon, his favorite spot to be with her. Even more than the library, although that had proved diverting.

"What are you doing?" She slid her arms around his neck and bent down to kiss his ear.

"Thinking about you." He could tell her that now, now that he'd told her he loved her. It felt marvelous to feel, to be able to share with her just what he was thinking. Especially when he was thinking about having her.

"What specifically are you thinking about?" she continued, sliding her mouth down his neck to his collarbone, licking him just there as her hands slid down his chest.

He reached up and folded his arms over hers, leaning his head back so she could reach more of him.

"Nothing specific," he said, closing his eyes as her hands ran their way over his chest, down his sides, and then lower still.

His wife was a vixen, that was for sure.

"Perhaps you could ponder what you might want to name a little girl or boy, then," she said, her voice muffled as she licked his neck.

He felt his eyes widen, and his hands tightened on her arms.

"Do you mean…?"

"Mm-hm," she said. "We're going to have a baby. Or rather, I am going to have a baby," his ever literal wife added. "You helped make the baby, of course, but all the rest of the work is up to me." He knew, without seeing her face, that she was wrinkling her nose. "Although why that is fair, I don't know. It is pleasurable to make the baby, and I can't imagine it will be nearly as much fun to actually have the baby. If there were a way…"

But she had to stop speaking then, because he stood up and wrapped her in his arms and kissed her until she was breathless.

If you loved this novella, you won't want to miss
the first in the Dukes Behaving Badly series,

A Duke's Guide to Correct Behavior,

ON SALE NOW!

And as a special bonus,
continue reading for a teaser from the next
Dukes Behaving Badly novel,

Put Up Your Duke,

ON SALE JUNE 30, 2015!

An Excerpt from

Put Up Your Duke

*1842, London, the Gentleman's Pleasure House,
Second Private Chamber on the Right*

"And then what will you do to me?" Nicholas didn't care so much for the particulars of the response—he knew the woman currently sitting on his lap would do what he wanted her to, and he would be gentlemanly enough to ensure she found enjoyment as well.

He was a very egalitarian lover.

"What do you want me to do to you?" she countered.

Clearly, she did not know that when he asked a question, he wanted an answer, not another question. He suppressed the feeling of irritation, and yes, boredom, and concentrated instead on placing a strawberry onto her breast, then lowering his mouth to capture the succulent fruit. Of the strawberry, not her breast. That appetizing treat would be for later.

He put his mouth to her ear and spoke so that neither of the two ladies, one on either side of him, could hear. "I want to keep your mouth busy so you can't speak. And when you are able to speak, you'll be screaming my name."

She wriggled on his lap, her plush arse riding his cock, which had already jerked to attention. She leaned her head back on his shoulder. "I've heard about you, m'lord, and I am very eager to find out if what they say is true."

Nicholas wrapped his hands around her waist and slid his thumbs up so they were in the soft crease under her breasts.

This was his favorite part of being with a woman—the anticipation, wondering what her face would look like as she came apart, wondering how her body would feel under his hands, how she'd want him to take her. The actual doing of it, well, that was pleasurable as well, but he hadn't found any of the women he'd been with had lived up to his expectations.

But each time, with each new woman, he hoped this would be the one. This female would be able to send him to a new height of ecstasy, of wanting, of being able to lose himself, forget thinking just for a few moments of bliss, who would be equal to him in bed, in conversation, in life.

Not that he thought he'd find that kind of woman here, in a house of ill repute, no matter how well it catered to men of his class. But he wasn't particularly interested in courting a young lady of his own class only to find, once he was married, that she was no true companion to him in bed or in conversation but that he was now married to her for life.

He'd considered it very seriously when he'd met a lady a year or so ago, but she'd entered into another engagement before he could figure out if he actually wanted to or not. So he remained single, and singly determined not to be wed, at least not unless he was absolutely certain about the wife in question.

But he wasn't going to eschew the pleasures of the bed just because he was pessimistic about his chances for long-term happiness. Short-term happiness, for now, would suit him just fine.

It seemed that other gentlemen in London felt the same way; the house was stocked with lovely women, rather like a well-tended fishpond, and it was as easy to catch one as baiting a hook. A hook made of money and a few well-chosen words. He had both in abundance, which was why he currently had three women surrounding him.

He was in one of the more opulent chambers, not on the enormous bed that dominated the room but instead seated on a long, low sofa upholstered in a dark purple hue. The furniture was also dark, and there were candles placed on several of the surfaces, and their light cast a warm, sensuous glow in the room. As though Nicholas and three willing ladies were not sensuous enough.

"M'lord?" The woman had turned in his lap so she faced him, while the other two women, women he'd had before, both of whom were quite skilled and enthusiastic, ruffled his hair and ran their fingers down his chest and murmured soft words, mostly involving him and them and what they were all going to do together later.

He was quite looking forward to it.

So he was not so happy when he heard his brother Griffith calling his name.

Griff wasn't bad, as brothers went; in fact, Nicholas quite liked him. But Griff, unlike his older brother, did not habituate houses of ill repute—or even houses of good repute—instead usually staying in the library to spend more time reading.

"Excuse me, ladies," Nicholas said, removing the woman from his lap and placing her gently beside him on the sofa. He did up the buttons of his shirt and ran a hand through his hair, which he knew was entirely disheveled, thanks to the sensual stroking and playing that had been done to it.

"In here, Griff," he shouted, getting to his feet. He was just tucking his shirt back into his trousers when Griffith entered, his brother's eyes widening as he saw what must have appeared to be absolute and total debauchery in the room.

Or, as Nicholas liked to call it, Tuesday.

"What is it?" he asked, since Griff's mouth was opening and closing like a chiming cuckoo clock.

"Here." Griff thrust a piece of paper at him. "I don't think you'd believe me if I just told you."

Nicholas unfolded the paper, heavy parchment that already gave whatever was written on it more weight than he wanted. He scanned the lines, filled with legal jargon, and then raised his head to stare at his brother. "This says...this makes me—"

Griff nodded. "The Duke of Gage."

Nicholas looked back at the paper, as though it would explain it all. Well, it did, actually, but he couldn't comprehend all the "whereases," "in testimony," and "further reviews."

"This can't...but how?" He looked at his brother, as though he could explain it.

"It seems that there was a dispute of lineage in a different branch of our family, quite remote, but the end result is that the current Duke of Gage isn't really, because a few generations up there was some bigamy." His brother could explain it. Excellent.

Only now—

"And the dukedom or whatever it is called goes to me? What about all the other relatives who were next in line?"

Griff shook his head. "That bigamous marriage affected many of the offspring. It's just like the War of the Roses, which began because John of Gaunt made his mistress his wife, and then that made their children not bastards, only—"

Nicholas punched his brother on the shoulder, not hard, just enough to make him stop talking. "I don't need a history lesson, and I sure as hell hope this doesn't result in a war."

"Right. Of course." Griff grinned and rubbed his shoulder. "Better you than me, I have to say."

Nicholas raised an eyebrow. "Well, if it were you, it would mean I was dead, so yes, I'm very glad it was me. So what do I do now?"

Griff shrugged. "The current duke is contesting the finding, of course, but it seems as though the legality of it is on your side. Or the illegality, rather."

Nicholas frowned. "And how is it that you know about this first, rather than me?"

Now his brother looked embarrassed. "Well, the solicitor came to the house, only you weren't there. And I thought you'd want to know right away."

Right. Because he was here, while his brother was at their shared abode, no doubt doing something worthy with his life rather than keeping company with no fewer than three loose women at a time. Unless that really was a worthy endeavor, and everyone in the world was wrong about suitable pursuits.

Not for the first time, Nicholas wondered just how it came to be that he and his brother were so different, yet so close. Griffith was happiest when his nose was buried in a book, while Nicholas was happiest when his nose was buried in a breast, preferably two.

His older sisters, both of whom were married, were entirely respectable as well, but they were only his half-sisters, so they didn't count as much.

He turned to the women, who were busy with each other. He had a pang as he saw just what one of them was doing to the other one, while the third watched, her eyes heavy with desire.

"It seems, my fair companions, that I have some urgent business that requires my attention."

All three of them paused to look at him, disappointment creeping over their expressions. The one in the middle, he thought her name was Sally, said in a pouting tone, "Are you sure? Your friend there could join us, just for a little while."

Nicholas glanced at Griff, whose face had turned an alarming shade of red. If it got any darker, he would match the sofa, in fact.

"I wish we could stay, ladies, but we have to go." He didn't want Griff to explode in some sort of embarrassed lust conflagration. That would be difficult to explain to their relatives.

He didn't wait for any response, just took Griff's arm and led him out the door, dropping a few coins into the hands of the woman who ran the establishment.

"So early?" she remarked, tucking the coins into her pocket. "We'll see you soon, my lord?"

Nicholas shook his head. "I regret to say I doubt I will be returning, at least not for some time. It appears I have a dukedom to inherit."

And with that, he pushed the door open and stepped out into the foggy night, his brother right behind.

ABOUT THE AUTHOR

MEGAN FRAMPTON writes historical romance under her own name and romantic women's fiction as Megan Caldwell. She likes the color black, gin, dark-haired British men, and huge earrings, not in that order. She lives in Brooklyn, New York, with her husband and son. You can visit her website at www.meganframpton.com. She tweets as @meganf and is at Facebook at facebook.com/meganframptonbooks.

Discover great authors, exclusive offers, and more at hc.com.

Give in to your impulses . . .
Read on for a sneak peek at seven brand-new
e-book original tales of romance
from HarperCollins.
Available now wherever e-books are sold.

VARIOUS STATES OF UNDRESS: GEORGIA

By Laura Simcox

MAKE IT LAST

A BOWLER UNIVERSITY NOVEL

By Megan Erickson

HERO BY NIGHT

BOOK THREE: INDEPENDENCE FALLS

By Sara Jane Stone

MAYHEM

By Jamie Shaw

SINFUL REWARDS 1
A BILLIONAIRES AND BIKERS NOVELLA
By Cynthia Sax

FORBIDDEN
AN UNDER THE SKIN NOVEL
By Charlotte Stein

HER HIGHLAND FLING
A NOVELLA
By Jennifer McQuiston

An Excerpt from

VARIOUS STATES OF UNDRESS: GEORGIA

by *Laura Simcox*

Laura Simcox concludes her fun, flirty
Various States of Undress series with a
presidential daughter, a hot baseball player,
and a tale of love at the ballgame.

"Uh. Hi."

Georgia splayed her hand over the front of her wet blouse and stared. The impossibly tanned guy standing just inside the doorway—wearing a tight T-shirt, jeans, and a smile—was as still as a statue. A statue with fathomless, unblinking chocolate brown eyes. She let her gaze drop from his face to his broad chest. "Oh. Hello. I was expecting someone else."

He didn't comment, but when she lifted her gaze again, past his wide shoulders and carved chin, she watched his smile turn into a grin, revealing way-too-sexy brackets at the corners of his mouth. He walked down the steps and onto the platform where she stood. He had to be at least 6'3", and testosterone poured off him like heat waves on the field below. She shouldn't stare at him, right? Damn. Her gaze flicked from him to the glass wall but moved right back again.

"Scared of heights?" he asked. His voice was a slow, deep Southern drawl. Sexy deep. "Maybe you oughta sit down."

"No, thanks. I was just . . . looking for something."

Looking for something? Like what—a tryst with a stranger in the press box? Her face heated, and she clutched the water bottle, the plastic making a snapping sound under her fingers. "So . . . how did you get past my agents?"

He smiled again. "They know who I am."

"And you are?"

"Brett Knox."

His name sounded familiar. "Okay. I'm Georgia Fulton. It's nice to meet you," she said, putting down her water.

He shook her hand briefly. "You, too. But I just came up here to let you know that I'm declining the interview. Too busy."

Georgia felt herself nodding in agreement, even as she realized *exactly* who Brett Knox was. He was the star catcher—and right in front of her, shooting her down before she'd even had a chance to ask. Such a typical jock.

"I'm busy, too, which is why I'd like to set up a time that's convenient for both of us," she said, even though she hoped it wouldn't be necessary. But she couldn't very well walk into the news station without accomplishing what she'd been tasked with—pinning him down. Georgia was a team player. So was Brett, literally.

"I don't want to disappoint my boss, and I'm betting you feel the same way about yours," she continued.

"Sure. I sign autographs, pose for photos, visit Little League teams. Like I said, I'm busy."

"That's nice." She nodded. "I'm flattered that you found the time to come all the way up to the press box and tell me, in person, that you don't have time for an interview. Thanks."

He smiled a little. "You're welcome." Then he stretched, his broad chest expanding with the movement. He flexed his long fingers, braced a hand high on the post, and grinned at her again. Her heart flipped down into her stomach. Oh, no.

"I get it, you know. I've posed for photos and signed autographs, too. I've visited hospitals and ribbon cutting ceremonies, and I know it makes people happy. But public appearances can be draining, and it takes time away from work. Right?"

"Right." He gave her a curious look. "We have that in common, though it's not exactly the same. I may be semifamous in Memphis, but I don't have paparazzi following me around, and I like it that way. You interviewing me would turn into a big hassle."

"I won't take much of your time. Just think of me as another reporter." She ventured a warm, inviting smile, and Brett's dark eyes widened. "The paparazzi don't follow me like they do my sisters. I'm the boring one."

"Really?" He folded his arms across his lean middle, and his gaze traveled slowly over her face.

She felt her heart speed up. "Yes, really."

"I beg to differ."

Before she could respond, he gave her another devastating smile and jogged up the steps. It was the best view she'd had all day. When Brett disappeared, she collapsed back against the post. He was right, of course. She wasn't just another reporter; she was the president's brainy daughter—who secretly lusted after athletes. And she'd just met a hell of an athlete.

Talk about a hot mess.

An Excerpt from

MAKE IT LAST
A Bowler University Novel
by Megan Erickson

The last installment in Megan Erickson's daringly
sexy Bowler University series finds Cam Ruiz
back in his hometown of Paradise, where he comes
face-to-face with the only girl he ever loved.

Cam sighed, feeling the weight of responsibility pressing down on his shoulders. But if he didn't help his mom, who would?

He jingled his keys in his pocket and turned to walk toward his truck. It was nice of Max and Lea to visit him on their road trip. College had been some of the best years of his life. Great friends, fun parties, hot girls.

But now it felt like a small blip, like a week vacation instead of three and a half years. And now he was right back where he started.

As he walked by the alley beside the restaurant, something flickered out of the corner of his eye.

He turned and spotted her legs first. One foot bent at the knee and braced on the brick wall, the other flat on the ground. Her head was bent, a curtain of hair blocking her face. But he knew those legs. He knew those hands. And he knew that hair, a light brown that held just a glint of strawberry in the sun. He knew by the end of August it'd be lighter and redder and she'd laugh about that time she put lemon juice in it. It'd backfired and turned her hair orange.

The light flickered again but it was something weird and artificial, not like the menthols she had smoked. Back when he knew her.

As she lowered her hand down to her side, he caught sight of the small white cylinder. It was an electronic cigarette. She'd quit.

She raised her head then, like she knew someone watched her, and he wanted to keep walking, avoid this awkward moment. Avoid those eyes he didn't think he'd ever see again and never thought he'd wanted to see again. But now that his eyes locked on her hazel eyes—the ones he knew began as green on the outside of her iris and darkened to brown by the time they met her pupil—he couldn't look away. His boots wouldn't move.

The small cigarette fell to the ground with a soft click and she straightened, both her feet on the ground.

And that was when he noticed the wedge shoes. And the black apron. What was she doing here?

"Camilo."

Other than his mom, she was the only one who used his full name. He'd heard her say it while laughing. He'd her moan it while he was inside her. He'd heard her sigh it with an eye roll when he made a bad joke. But he'd never heard it the way she said it now, with a little bit of fear and anxiety and . . . longing? He took a deep breath to steady his voice. "Tatum."

He hadn't spoken her name since that night Trevor called him and told him what she did. The night the future that he'd set out for himself and for her completely changed course.

She'd lost some weight in the four years since he'd last seen her. He'd always loved her curves. She had it all—thighs, ass and tits in abundance. Naked, she was a fucking vision.

Damn it, he wasn't going there.

But now her face looked thinner, her clothes hung a little loose and he didn't like this look as much. Not that she probably gave a fuck about his opinion anymore.

She still had her gorgeous hair, pinned up halfway with a bump in front, and a smattering of freckles across the bridge of her nose and on her cheekbones. And she still wore her makeup exactly the same—thickly mascaraed eyelashes, heavy eyeliner that stretched to a point on the outside of her eyes, like a modern-day Audrey Hepburn.

She was still beautiful. And she still took his breath away.

And his heart felt like it was breaking all over again.

And he hated her even more for that.

Her eyes were wide. "What are you doing here?"

Something in him bristled at that. Maybe it was because he didn't feel like he belonged here. But then, she didn't either. She never did. *They* never did.

But there was no longer a *they.*

An Excerpt from

HERO BY NIGHT
Book Three: Independence Falls
by Sara Jane Stone

Travel back to Independence Falls in Sara Jane Stone's next thrilling read. Armed with a golden retriever and a concealed weapons permit, Lena Clark is fighting for normal. She served her country, but the experience left her afraid to be touched and estranged from her career-military family. Staying in Independence Falls, and finding a job, seems like the first step to reclaiming her life and preparing for the upcoming medal ceremony— until the town playboy stumbles into her bed . . .

Sometimes beauty knocked a man on his ass, leaving him damn near desperate for a taste, a touch, and hopefully a round or two between the sheets—or tied up in them. The knockout blonde with the large golden retriever at her feet took the word "beautiful" to a new level.

Chad Summers stared at her, unable to look away or dim the smile on his face. He usually masked his interest better, stopping short of looking like he was begging for it before learning a woman's name. But this mysterious beauty had special written all over her.

She stared at him, her gaze open and wanting. For a heartbeat. Then she turned away, her back to the party as she stared out at Eric Moore's pond.

Her hair flowed in long waves down her back. One look left him wishing he could wrap his hand around her shiny locks and pull. His gaze traveled over her back, taking in the outline of gentle curves beneath her flowing, and oh-so-feminine, floor-length dress. The thought of the beauty's long skirt decorating her waist propelled him into motion. Chad headed in her direction, moving away from the easy, quiet conversation about God-knew-what on the patio.

The blonde, a mysterious stranger in a sea of familiar faces, might be the spark this party needed. He was a few feet away when the dog abandoned his post at her side and cut Chad off. Either the golden retriever was protecting his owner, or the animal was in cahoots with the familiar voice calling his name.

"Chad Summers!"

The blonde turned at the sound, looking first at him, her blue eyes widening as if surprised at how close he stood, and then at her dog. From the other direction, a familiar face with short black hair—Susan maybe?—marched toward him.

Without a word, Maybe Susan stopped by his side and raised her glass. With a dog in front of him, trees to one side, and an angry woman on his other, there was no escape.

"Hi there." He left off her name just in case he'd guessed wrong, but offered a warm, inviting smile. Most women fell for that grin, but if Maybe Susan had at one time—and seeing her up close, she looked very familiar, though he could swear he'd never slept with her—she wasn't falling for it today.

She poured the cool beer over his head, her mouth set in a firm line. "That was for my sister. Susan Lewis? You spent the night with her six months ago and never called."

Chad nodded, silently grateful he hadn't addressed the pissed-off woman by her sister's name. "My apologies, ma'am."

"You're a dog," Susan's sister announced. The animal at his feet stepped forward as if affronted by the comparison.

"For the past six months, my little sister has talked about you, saving every article about your family's company," the angry woman continued.

Whoa . . . Yes, he'd taken Susan Lewis out once and they'd ended the night back at his place, but he could have sworn they were on the same page. Hell, he'd heard her say the words, *I'm not looking for anything serious*, and he'd believed her. It was one freaking night. He didn't think he needed signed documents that spelled out his intentions and hers.

"She's practically built a shrine to you," she added, waving her empty beer cup. "Susan was ready to plan your wedding."

"Again, I'm sorry, but it sounds like there was a miscommunication." Chad withdrew a bandana from his back pocket, one that had belonged to his father, and wiped his brow. "But wedding bells are not in my future. At least not anytime soon."

The angry sister shook her head, spun on her heels, and marched off.

Chad turned to the blonde and offered a grin. She looked curious, but not ready to run for the hills. "I guess I made one helluva first impression."

"Hmm." She glanced down at her dog as if seeking comfort in the fact that he stood between them.

"I'm Chad Summers." He held out his hand—the one part of his body not covered in beer.

"You're Katie's brother." She glanced briefly at his extended hand, but didn't take it.

He lowered his arm, still smiling. "Guilty."

"Lena." She nodded to the dog. "That's Hero."

"Nice to meet you both." He looked up the hill. Country music drifted down from the house. Someone had finally added some life to the party. Couples moved to the beat on the blue stone patio, laughing and drinking under the clear Oregon night sky. In the corner, Liam Trulane tossed logs into a fire pit.

"After I dry off," Chad said, turning back to the blonde, "how about a dance?"

"No."

An Excerpt from

MAYHEM

by Jamie Shaw

A straitlaced college freshman is drawn
to a sexy and charismatic rock star in this
fabulous debut New Adult novel for fans
of Jamie McGuire and Jay Crownover!

"**I** can't believe I let you talk me into this." I tug at the black hem of the stretchy nylon skirt my best friend squeezed me into, but unless I want to show the top of my panties instead of the skin of my thighs, there's nothing I can do. After casting yet another uneasy glance at the long line of people stretched behind me on the sidewalk, I shift my eyes back to the sun-warmed fabric pinched between my fingers and grumble, "The least you could've done was let me wear some leggings."

I look like Dee's closet drank too much and threw up on me. She somehow talked me into wearing this mini-skirt—which skintight doesn't even begin to describe—and a hot-pink top that shows more cleavage than should be legal. The front of it drapes all the way down to just above my navel, and the bottom exposes a pale sliver of skin between the hem of the shirt and the top of my skirt. The fabric matches my killer hot-pink heels.

Literally, killer. Because I know I'm going to fall on my face and die.

I'm fiddling with the skirt again when one of the guys near us in line leans in close, a jackass smile on his lips. "I think you look hot."

"I have a boyfriend," I counter, but Dee just scoffs at me.

"She means *thank you*," she shoots back, chastising me with her tone until the guy flashes us another arrogant smile—he's stuffed into an appallingly snug graphic-print tee that might as well say "douche bag" in its shiny metallic lettering, and even Dee can't help but make a face before we both turn away.

She and I are the first ones in line for the show tonight, standing by the doors to Mayhem under the red-orange glow of a setting summer sun. She's been looking forward to this night for weeks, but I was more excited about it before my boyfriend of three years had to back out.

"Brady is a jerk," she says, and all I can do is sigh because I wish those two could just get along. Deandra and I have been best friends since preschool, but Brady and I have been dating since my sophomore year of high school and living together for the past two months. "He should be here to appreciate how gorgeous you look tonight, but nooo, it's always work first with him."

"He moved all the way here to be with me, Dee. Cut him some slack, all right?"

She grumbles her frustration until she catches me touching my eyelids for the zillionth time tonight. Yanking my fingers away, she orders, "Stop messing with it. You'll smear."

I stare down at my shadowy fingertips and rub them together. "Tell me the truth," I say, flicking the clumped powder away. "Do I look like a clown?"

"You look smoking hot!" she assures me with a smile.

I finally feel like I'm beginning to loosen up when a guy walks right past us like he's going to cut in line. In dark shades and a baggy black knit cap that droops in the back, he flicks a cigarette to the ground, and my eyes narrow on him.

Dee and I have been waiting for way too long to let some self-entitled jerk cut in front of us, so when he knocks on the door to the club, I force myself to speak up.

"They're not letting people in yet," I say, hoping he takes the hint. Even with my skyscraper heels, I feel dwarfed standing next to him. He has to be at least six-foot-two, maybe taller.

He turns his head toward me and lowers his shades, smirking like something's funny. His wrist is covered with string bracelets and rubber bracelets and a thick leather cuff, and three of his fingernails on each hand are painted black. But his eyes are what steal the words from my lips—a greenish shade of light gray. They're stunning.

When the door opens, he turns back to it and locks hands with the bouncer.

"You're late," the bouncer says, and the guy in the shades laughs and slips inside. Once he disappears, Dee pushes my shoulders.

"Oh my GOD! Do you know who you were just talking to?!"

I shake my head.

"That was *Adam* EVEREST! He's the lead singer of the band we're here to see!"

An Excerpt from

SINFUL REWARDS 1
A Billionaires and Bikers Novella
by Cynthia Sax

Belinda "Bee" Carter is a good girl; at least, that's
what she tells herself. And a good girl deserves
a nice guy—just like the gorgeous and moody
billionaire Nicolas Rainer. Or so she thinks,
until she takes a look through her telescope
and sees a naked, tattooed man on the balcony
across the courtyard. He has been watching
her, and that makes him all the more enticing.
But when a mysterious and anonymous text
message dares her to do something bad, she
must decide if she is really the good girl she has
always claimed to be, or if she's willing to risk
everything for her secret fantasy of being watched.

An Avon Red Impulse Novella

I'd told Cyndi I'd never use it, that it was an instrument purchased by perverts to spy on their neighbors. She'd laughed and called me a prude, not knowing that I was one of those perverts, that I secretly yearned to watch and be watched, to care and be cared for.

If I'm cautious, and I'm always cautious, she'll never realize I used her telescope this morning. I swing the tube toward the bench and adjust the knob, bringing the mysterious object into focus.

It's a phone. Nicolas's phone. I bounce on the balls of my feet. This is a sign, another declaration from fate that we belong together. I'll return Nicolas's much-needed device to him. As a thank you, he'll invite me to dinner. We'll talk. He'll realize how perfect I am for him, fall in love with me, marry me.

Cyndi will find a fiancé also—everyone loves her—and we'll have a double wedding, as sisters of the heart often do. It'll be the first wedding my family has had in generations.

Everyone will watch us as we walk down the aisle. I'll wear a strapless white Vera Wang mermaid gown with organza and lace details, crystal and pearl embroidery accents, the bodice fitted, and the skirt hemmed for my shorter height. My hair will be swept up. My shoes—

Voices murmur outside the condo's door, the sound piercing my delightful daydream. I swing the telescope upward, not wanting to be caught using it. The snippets of conversation drift away.

I don't relax. If the telescope isn't positioned in the same way as it was last night, Cyndi will realize I've been using it. She'll tease me about being a fellow pervert, sharing the story, embellished for dramatic effect, with her stern, serious dad—or, worse, with Angel, that snobby friend of hers.

I'll die. It'll be worse than being the butt of jokes in high school because that ridicule was about my clothes and this will center on the part of my soul I've always kept hidden. It'll also be the truth, and I won't be able to deny it. I am a pervert.

I have to return the telescope to its original position. This is the only acceptable solution. I tap the metal tube.

Last night, my man-crazy roommate was giggling over the new guy in three-eleven north. The previous occupant was a gray-haired, bowtie-wearing tax auditor, his luxurious accommodations supplied by Nicolas. The most exciting thing he ever did was drink his tea on the balcony.

According to Cyndi, the new occupant is a delicious piece of man candy—tattooed, buff, and head-to-toe lickable. He was completing armcurls outside, and she enthusiastically counted his reps, oohing and aahing over his bulging biceps, calling to me to take a look.

I resisted that temptation, focusing on making macaroni and cheese for the two of us, the recipe snagged from the diner my mom works in. After we scarfed down dinner, Cyndi licking her plate clean, she left for the club and hasn't returned.

Three-eleven north is the mirror condo to ours. I

straighten the telescope. That position looks about right, but then, the imitation UGGs I bought in my second year of college looked about right also. The first time I wore the boots in the rain, the sheepskin fell apart, leaving me barefoot in Economics 201.

Unwilling to risk Cyndi's friendship on "about right," I gaze through the eyepiece. The view consists of rippling golden planes, almost like . . .

Tanned skin pulled over defined abs.

I blink. It can't be. I take another look. A perfect pearl of perspiration clings to a puckered scar. The drop elongates more and more, stretching, snapping. It trickles downward, navigating the swells and valleys of a man's honed torso.

No. I straighten. This is wrong. I shouldn't watch our sexy neighbor as he stands on his balcony. If anyone catches me . . .

Parts 1 – 7 available now!

An Excerpt from

FORBIDDEN
An Under the Skin Novel
by Charlotte Stein

Killian is on the verge of making his final vows
for the priesthood when he saves Dorothy from a
puritanical and oppressive home. The attraction
between them is swift and undeniable, but every
touch, every glance, every moment of connection
between them is completely forbidden . . .

An Avon Red Impulse Novel

We get out of the car at this swanky-looking place called Marriott, with a big promise next to the door about all-day breakfasts and internet and other stuff I've never had in my whole life, all these nice cars in the parking lot gleaming in the dimming light and a dozen windows lit up like some Christmas card, and then it just happens. My excitement suddenly bursts out of my chest, and before I can haul it back in, it runs right down the length of my arm, all the way to my hand.

Which grabs hold of his, so tight it could never be mistaken for anything else.

Course I want it to be mistaken for anything else, as soon as he looks at me. His eyes snap to my face like I poked him in the ribs with a rattler snake, and just in case I'm in any doubt, he glances down at the thing I'm doing. He sees me touching him as though he's not nearly a priest and I'm not under his care, and instead we're just two people having some kind of happy honeymoon.

In a second we're going inside to have all the sex.

That's what it seems like—like a sex thing.

I can't even explain it away as just being friendly, because somehow it doesn't feel friendly at all. My palm has been laced with electricity, and it just shot ten thousand volts into him. His whole body has gone tense, and so my body goes tense, but the worst part about it is:

For some ungodly reason he doesn't take his hand away.

Maybe he thinks if he does it will look bad, like admitting to a guilty thing that neither of us has done. Or at least that he hasn't done. He didn't ask to have his hand grabbed. His hand is totally innocent in all of this. My hand is the evil one. It keeps right on grasping him even after I tell it to stop. I don't even care if it makes me look worse—*just let go*, I think at it.

But the hand refuses.

It still has him in its evil clutches when we go inside the motel. My fingers are starting to sweat, and the guy behind the counter is noticing, yet I can't seem to do a single thing about it. Could be we have to spend the rest of our lives like this, out of sheer terror at drawing any attention to the thing I have done.

Unless he's just carrying on because he thinks I'm scared of this place. Maybe he thinks I need comfort, in which case all of this might be okay. I am just a girl with her friendly, good-looking priest, getting a motel room in a real honest and platonic way so I can wash my lank hair and secretly watch television about spaceships.

Nothing is going to happen—a fact that I communicate to the counter guy with my eyes. I don't know why I'm doing it, however. He doesn't know Killian is a priest. He has no clue that I'm some beat-up kid who needs help and protection rather than sordid hand-holding. He probably thinks we're married, just like I thought before, and the only thing that makes that idea kind of off is how I look in comparison.

I could pass for a stripe of beige paint next to him. In here his black hair is like someone took a slice out of the night sky. His cheekbones are so big and manly I could bludgeon the counter guy with them, and I'm liable to do it. He keeps staring, even after Killian says "two rooms please." He's still staring as we go down the carpeted hallway, to the point where I have to ask.

"Why was he looking like that?" I whisper as Killian fits a key that is not really a key but a gosh darn credit card into a room door. So of course I'm looking at that when he answers me, and not at his face.

But I wish I had been. I wish I'd seen his expression when he spoke, because when he did he said the single most startling thing I ever heard in my whole life.

"He was looking because you're lovely."

An Excerpt from

HER HIGHLAND FLING
A Novella
by Jennifer McQuiston

When his little Scottish town is in desperate
straits, William MacKenzie decides to resurrect
the Highland Games in an effort to take
advantage of the new tourism boom and invites
a London newspaper to report on the events.
He's prepared to show off for the sake of the
town, but the one thing William never expects
is for this intrepid reporter to be a she . . .

William scowled. Moraig's future was at stake. The town's economy was hardly prospering, and its weathered residents couldn't depend on fishing and gossip to sustain them forever. They needed a new direction, and as the Earl of Kilmartie's heir, he felt obligated to sort out a solution. He'd spent months organizing the upcoming Highland Games. It was a calculated risk that, if properly orchestrated, would ensure the betterment of every life in town. It had seemed a brilliant opportunity to reach those very tourists they were aiming to attract.

But with the sweat now pooling in places best left unmentioned and the minutes ticking slowly by, that brilliance was beginning to tarnish.

William peered down the road that led into town, imagining he could see a cloud of dust implying the arrival of the afternoon coach. The very *late* afternoon coach. But all he saw was the delicate shimmer of heat reflecting the nature of the devilishly hot day.

"Bugger it all," he muttered. "How late can a coach be? There's only one route from Inverness." He plucked at the damp collar of his shirt, wondering where the coachman could be. "Mr. Jeffers knew the importance of being on time

today. We need to make a ripping first impression on this reporter."

James's gaze dropped once more to William's bare legs.
"Oh, I don't think there's any doubt of it." He leaned against
the posthouse wall and crossed his arms. "If I might ask the
question . . . why turn it into such a circus? Why these Games
instead of, say, a well-placed rumor of a beastie living in Loch
Moraig? You've got the entire town in an uproar preparing
for it."

William could allow that James was perhaps a bit distracted by his pretty wife and new baby—and understand-
ably so. But given that his brother was raising his bairns here,
shouldn't he want to ensure Moraig's future success more
than anyone?

James looked up suddenly, shading his eyes with a hand.
"Well, best get those knees polished to a shine. There's your
coach now. Half hour late, as per usual."

With a near-groan of relief, William stood at attention on
the posthouse steps as the mail coach roared up in a choking
cloud of dust and hot wind.

A half hour off schedule. Perhaps it wasn't the tragedy
he'd feared. They could skip the initial stroll down Main
Street he'd planned and head straight to the inn. He could
point out some of the pertinent sights later, when he showed
the man the competition field that had been prepared on the
east side of town.

"And dinna tell the reporter I'm the heir," William warned
as an afterthought. "We want him to think of Moraig as a
charming and rustic retreat from London." If the town was to

have a future, it needed to be seen as a welcome escape from titles and peers and such, and he did not want this turning into a circus where he stood at the center of the ring.

As the coach groaned to a stop, James clapped William on the shoulder with mock sympathy. "Don't worry. With those bare legs, I suspect your reporter will have enough to write about without nosing about the details of your inheritance."

The coachman secured the reins and jumped down from his perch. A smile of amusement broke across Mr. Jeffers's broad features. "Wore the plaid today, did we?"

Bloody hell. Not Jeffers, too.

"You're late." William scowled. "Were there any problems fetching the chap from Inverness?" He was anxious to greet the reporter, get the man properly situated in the Blue Gander, and then go home to change into something less . . . *Scottish.* And God knew he could also use a pint or three, though preferably ones not raised at his expense.

Mr. Jeffers pushed the brim of his hat up an inch and scratched his head. "Well, see, here's the thing. I dinna exactly fetch a chap, as it were."

This time William couldn't suppress the growl that erupted from his throat. "Mr. Jeffers, don't tell me you *left* him there!" It would be a nightmare if he had. The entire thing was carefully orchestrated, down to a reservation for the best room the Blue Gander had to offer. The goal had been to install the reporter safely in Moraig and give him a taste of the town's charms *before* the Games commenced on Saturday.

"Well, I . . . that is . . ." Mr. Jeffers's gaze swung between them, and he finally shrugged. "Well, I suppose you'll see well enough for yourself."

He turned the handle, then swung the coach door open.

A gloved hand clasped Mr. Jeffers's palm, and then a high, elegant boot flashed into sight.

"What in the blazes—" William started to say, only to choke on his surprise as a blonde head dipped into view. A body soon followed, stepping down in a froth of blue skirts. She dropped Jeffers's hand and looked around with bright interest.

"Your chap's a lass," explained a bemused Mr. Jeffers.

"A lass?" echoed William stupidly.

And not only a lass . . . a very pretty lass.

She smiled at them, and it was like the sun cresting over the hills that rimmed Loch Moraig, warming all who were fortunate enough to fall in its path. He was suddenly and inexplicably consumed by the desire to recite poetry to the sound of twittering birds. That alone might have been manageable, but as her eyes met his, he was also consumed by an unfortunate jolt of lustful awareness that left no inch of him unscathed—and there were quite a few inches to cover.

"Miss Penelope Tolbertson," she said, extending her gloved hand as though she were a man. "R-reporter for the *London Times*."

He stared at her hand, unsure of whether to shake it or kiss it. Her manners might be bold, but her voice was like butter, flowing over his body until it didn't know which end was up. His tongue seemed wrapped in cotton, muffling even the merest hope of a proper greeting.

The reporter was female?

And not only female . . . a veritable goddess, with eyes the color of a fair Highland sky?

He raised his eyes to meet hers, giving himself up to the sense of falling.

Or perhaps more aptly put, a sense of flailing.

"W-welcome to Moraig, Miss Tolbertson."